FÜN學
美國英語閱讀課本
各學科實用課文 二版

+ Workbook

U0033666

AMERICAN
SCHOOL
TEXTBOOK
READING KEY

作者 Michael A. Putlack & e-Creative Contents　　譯者 丁宥暄

MP3
寂天雲 APP

如何下載 MP3 音檔

❶ 寂天雲 APP 聆聽：掃描書上 QR Code 下載「寂天雲－英日語學習隨身聽」APP。加入會員後，用 APP 內建掃描器再次掃描書上 QR Code，即可使用 APP 聆聽音檔。

❷ 官網下載音檔：請上「寂天閱讀網」（www.icosmos.com.tw），註冊會員／登入後，搜尋本書，進入本書頁面，點選「MP3 下載」下載音檔，存於電腦等其他播放器聆聽使用。

The Best Preparation for Building Academic Reading Skills and Vocabulary

The Reading Key series is designed to help students to understand American school textbooks and to develop background knowledge in a wide variety of academic topics. This series also provides learners with the opportunity to enhance their reading comprehension skills and vocabulary, which will assist them when they take various English exams.

Reading Key <Volume 1-3> is
a three-book series designed for beginner to intermediate learners.

Reading Key <Volume 4-6> is
a three-book series designed for intermediate to high-intermediate learners.

Reading Key <Volume 7-9> is
a three-book series designed for high-intermediate learners.

Features

- A wide variety of topics that cover American school subjects
  helps learners expand their knowledge of academic topics through interdisciplinary studies

- Intensive practice for reading skill development
  helps learners prepare for various English exams

- Building vocabulary by school subjects and themed texts
  helps learners expand their vocabulary and reading skills in each subject

- Graphic organizers for each passage
  show the structure of the passage and help to build summary skills

- Captivating pictures and illustrations related to the topics
  help learners gain a broader understanding of the topics and key concepts

Table of Contents

Chapter 1
Social Studies • History and Geography

Theme: **Geography Skills**
Unit 01 Reading Maps 8
Unit 02 Mountains, Rivers, and Deserts of the World 10

Theme: **The World Economy**
Unit 03 A World of Trade 12
Unit 04 Ancient Trade 14

Vocabulary Review 1 16

Theme: **Ancient Egypt**
Unit 05 The Gift of the Nile 18
Unit 06 The Culture of Egypt 20

Theme: **Ancient Greece**
Unit 07 Ancient Greece 22
Unit 08 Socrates and Plato 24

Vocabulary Review 2 26

Theme: **Ancient Rome**
Unit 09 Ancient Rome 28
Unit 10 The Founding of Rome 30

Theme: **The Middle Ages**
Unit 11 Europe in the Middle Ages 32
Unit 12 Feudalism 34

Vocabulary Review 3 36

Wrap-Up Test 1 38

Chapter 2
Science

Theme: **Inquiry Skills and Scientific Tools**
Unit 13 What Is the Scientific Method? 40
Unit 14 Scientific Tools 42

Theme: **A World of Living Things**
Unit 15 What Are Cells? 44
Unit 16 Classifying Living Things 46

Vocabulary Review 4 48

Theme: **Heredity and Traits**

Unit 17 What Is Heredity? 50

Unit 18 What Are Traits? 52

Theme: **The History of the Earth**

Unit 19 The Formation of the Earth 54

Unit 20 Continental Drift 56

Vocabulary Review 5 58

Theme: **Energy**

Unit 21 Light and Heat 60

Unit 22 Electricity 62

Theme: **Motion and Force**

Unit 23 Motion and Force 64

Unit 24 Simple Machines 66

Vocabulary Review 6 68

Wrap-Up Test 2 70

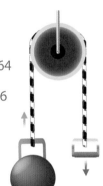

Chapter 3
Mathematics • Language •
Visual Arts • Music

Theme: **Fractions**

Unit 25 Understanding Fractions 72

Unit 26 Word Problems With Fractions 74

Theme: **Geometry**

Unit 27 Lines and Angles 76

Unit 28 Polygons, Triangles, and Circles 78

Vocabulary Review 7 80

Theme: **Learning About Language**

Unit 29 Prefixes and Suffixes 82

Unit 30 Tenses 84

Theme: **Grammar**

Unit 31 Complete Sentences 86

Unit 32 Proofreading 88

Vocabulary Review 8 90

Theme: **Visual Arts**

Unit 33 The Art of the Middle Ages 92

Unit 34 The Art of Islam and Africa 94

Theme: **A World of Music**

Unit 35 Musical Notation 96

Unit 36 Composers and Their Music 98

Vocabulary Review 9 100

Wrap-Up Test 3 102

• Word List 104

• Answers and Translations 112

Workbook for Daily Review

Syllabus Vol. 6

Subject	Topic & Area	Title
Social Studies ★ **History and Geography**	World Geography	Reading Maps
	World Geography	Mountains, Rivers, and Deserts of the World
	Economics	A World of Trade
	Economics	Ancient Trade
	World History	The Gift of the Nile
	World History	The Culture of Egypt
	World History	Ancient Greece
	World History	Socrates and Plato
	World History	Ancient Rome
	World History	The Founding of Rome
	World History	Europe in the Middle Ages
	World History	Feudalism
Science	What Is Science?	What Is the Scientific Method?
	What Is Science?	Scientific Tools
	A World of Living Things	What Are Cells?
	A World of Living Things	Classifying Living Things
	Heredity	What Is Heredity?
	Heredity	What Are Traits?
	Our Earth	The Formation of the Earth
	Our Earth	Continental Drift
	Energy	Light and Heat
	Energy	Electricity
	Motion and Force	Motion and Force
	Motion and Force	Simple Machines
Mathematics	Fractions	Understanding Fractions
	Fractions	Word Problems With Fractions
	Geometry	Lines and Angles
	Geometry	Polygons, Triangles, and Circles
Language and Literature	Language Arts	Prefixes and Suffixes
	Language Arts	Tenses
	Language Arts	Complete Sentences
	Language Arts	Proofreading
Visual Arts	Visual Arts	The Art of the Middle Ages
	Visual Arts	The Art of Islam and Africa
Music	A World of Music	Musical Notation
	A World of Music	Composers and Their Music

1

- Social Studies
- History and Geography

There are many different kinds of maps.

Key Words

- territorial
- border
- landform
- rely on
- display
- occur
- focus on
- route
- locator

A political map shows where cities, states, and countries are located. Political maps use lines to show territorial borders, such as state and country borders.

A physical map shows landforms and bodies of water. Landforms are different types of land on the earth's surface. Bodies of water include oceans, rivers, and lakes. These maps rely on colors to display different geographical features. For instance, water is blue, mountains are brown, and forests are green. These maps are also called landform maps.

A historical map is a map that shows information about past events and where they occurred. Historical maps often have dates in their titles.

A road map and a transportation map focus on roads and streets. They show important buildings and transportation routes such as airports, railroads, and highways.

Sometimes, you can see a small map set onto the main map. We call it a "locator" or "locator map." It shows where the area of the main map is located.

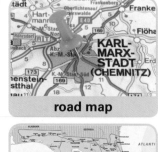

road map

 Different Kinds of Maps

political map

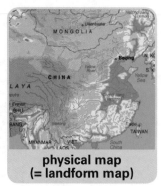

**physical map
(= landform map)**

historical map

**locator map
(= locator)**

Main Idea and Details

1 **What is the main idea of the passage?**

    a. Political maps are very useful.   **b.** There are many kinds of maps.

    c. Physical maps show different landforms.

2 **A _____ is a small map that is set onto the main map.**

    a. locator   **b.** transportation route   **c.** landform

3 **What color are mountains on a physical map?**

    a. Green.   **b.** Brown.   **c.** Blue.

4 **What does display mean?**

    a. Focus.   **b.** Show.   **c.** Locate.

5 **Complete the sentences.**

    a. Lines on political maps may show the _____ between countries.

    b. A _____ map may have dates in its title.

    c. Airports, railroads, and _____ may appear on a road map.

6 **Complete the outline.**

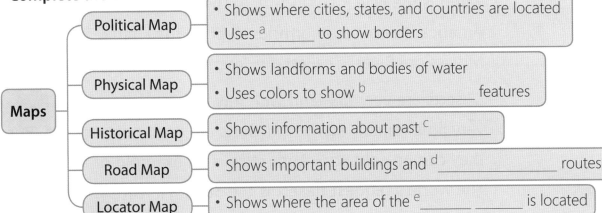

Maps

- **Political Map**
  - Shows where cities, states, and countries are located
  - Uses ª_____ to show borders
- **Physical Map**
  - Shows landforms and bodies of water
  - Uses colors to show ᵇ_____ features
- **Historical Map**
  - Shows information about past ᶜ_____
- **Road Map**
  - Shows important buildings and ᵈ_____ routes
- **Locator Map**
  - Shows where the area of the ᵉ_____ is located

Vocabulary Builder

Write the correct word and the meaning in Chinese.

 **1** ▸ relating to the land of a particular country

_____

 **2** ▸ a line that divides one state or country from another

_____

 **3** ▸ pay particular attention to

_____

 **4** ▸ a smaller map set onto the main map that shows the "big picture" of a place

_____

Mountains, Rivers, and Deserts of the World

Key Words

- steep
- mountain range
- mountain chain
- peak
- flow into
- source
- tributary
- empty into
- mighty
- arid

Mountains are high landforms with steep sides. They often form mountain ranges or mountain chains. The Himalaya Mountains are in Asia. Mt. Everest, the world's highest mountain, and many other high peaks are located there. In Europe, there are the Alps. South America has the Andes Mountains. And North America has the Appalachians and the Rocky Mountains.

Rivers are long streams of water that flow into another body of water. Their source—the starting place of a river—may be high in a mountain. Then, they flow until they reach the sea. Many tributaries also empty into large rivers. The longest river in the world is the Nile River in Africa. The Amazon River in South America is another enormous river. In the United States, the Mississippi River is called the "mighty Mississippi."

Deserts are very dry land with few plants and animals. They get very little rainfall, so most deserts are both hot and arid. But they can be cold, too. Antarctica is an example of a cold desert. The world's biggest desert is the Sahara in Africa. Next is the Arabian Desert in the Middle East. The Gobi Desert in Asia is another huge desert.

Mt. Everest

the world's highest mountain

Nile River

the world's longest river

Sahara Desert

the world's biggest desert

Main Idea and Details

1 **What is the passage mainly about?**

  a. Some of the world's important rivers.　　**b.** The biggest deserts on the earth.

  c. Some enormous landforms on the earth.

2 _____ **is a big river in South America.**

  a. The Mississippi River　　**b.** The Nile River　　**c.** The Amazon River

3 **Which mountain chain is found in Europe?**

  a. The Rocky Mountains.　　**b.** The Alps.　　**c.** The Andes Mountains.

4 **What does empty mean?**

  a. Create.　　**b.** Flow.　　**c.** Remove.

5 **According to the passage, which statement is true?**

  a. The Himalayas are located in Africa.

  b. The longest river in the world is the Amazon.

  c. Antarctica is a desert.

6 **Complete the outline.**

Mountains, Rivers, and Deserts of the World

Mountains	Rivers	Deserts
• Are high landforms • The Himalayas = in ª_____ • The Alps = in Europe • The Andes = in South America • The Appalachians and the ᵇ_____ _____ = in North America	• Are long ᶜ_____ of water • The Nile = longest river • The Amazon = enormous river • The Mississippi = "ᵈ_____ Mississippi"	• Are dry land • Antarctica = cold desert • The ᵉ_____ = biggest desert • The Arabian Desert = next biggest desert • The Gobi = huge desert in Asia

Vocabulary Builder

Write the correct word and the meaning in Chinese.

1  ▸ very large, powerful, or impressive

_____

2  ▸ the starting place of a river

_____

3  ▸ a stream or river that flows into a larger river

_____

4  ▸ very dry

_____

We live in a globalized world. This means that every area on the planet is in contact with every other area. One way that people contact each other is through trade. Trade is the buying and selling of goods and services.

Trade between different countries is called international trade. Many companies try to sell their goods all around the world. When they send their goods to another country, they are exporting them. Many companies buy resources and other products from other countries as well. When they bring in goods from another country, they are importing them. Most countries try to export more than they import.

Many times, when goods are imported, the buyer must pay a tariff. A tariff is a tax that a government collects on imported goods. Trade that has no taxes or government interference is called free trade.

Many of the world's countries have free market economies. In a free market economy, people decide what to produce and what to buy. However, in some countries, the government controls what is bought and sold.

Key Words

- globalize
- planet
- in contact with
- trade
- international trade
- export
- import
- tariff
- collect
- interference
- free trade
- free market economy

International Trade

TO THE U.S.A.

United States

Taiwan

TO TAIWAN

Countries buy and sell goods and resources across international borders.

Main Idea and Details

1 **What is the main idea of the passage?**

    a. Countries want to export more goods than they import.

    b. Not every country in the world has a free market economy.

    c. People buy and sell goods and services all over the world.

2 _____ **is a tax on imported goods.**

    a. An import   **b.** An export   **c.** A tariff

3 **What is a free market economy?**

    a. An economy in which the government controls buying and selling.

    b. An economy in which people decide what to produce and buy.

    c. An economy in which people pay taxes on imported goods.

4 **What does controls mean?**

    a. Concentrates.   **b.** Trades.   **c.** Regulates.

5 **Answer the questions.**

    a. What is trade? _____

    b. What is international trade? _____

    c. What is free trade? _____

6 **Complete the outline.**

Trade

What It Is
- The buying and ^a_____ of goods and services

International Trade
- Trade between different ^b_____
- Export = to send goods to other countries
- Import = to ^c_____ in goods from other countries

Free Trade
- Trade with no tariffs or government interference
- Tariff = a ^d_____ on imported goods

Vocabulary Builder

Write the correct word and the meaning in Chinese.

 **1** ▸ to sell goods and resources to other countries

_____

 **2** ▸ to make (something) cover, involve, or affect the entire world

_____

 **3** ▸ trade that has no taxes or government interference

_____

 **4** ▸ the act of interfering

_____

Key Words

- benefit
- natural resources
- human resources
- communication
- cargo ship
- conduct
- pottery
- sail
- barter
- merchant
- Silk Road
- silk
- gem
- spice

Why do people trade? People trade with each other because they both benefit. Countries around the world have different natural resources and human resources. People in each country produce different goods using these resources. They trade these items for goods they do not produce. That is trade.

Thanks to transportation and communication, people around the world can trade more quickly today than ever before.

Long ago, people also traded with each other. Thousands of years ago, there were no cargo ships, airplanes, telephones, or computers. But people still conducted international trade.

For instance, people in ancient Greece used to trade with others around the Mediterranean Sea. Greeks made beautiful pottery and grew olives and grapes. They traded these items for goods they needed. Greek ships often sailed across the sea to Egypt. In Egypt, they bartered their products for cotton, fruit, and wheat.

The ancient Romans also traded for many goods with Egypt and other nearby countries. The Romans also traded with China and India. Merchants used a route called the Silk Road to go to China. They traded gold and farm goods for silk, gems, and spices from China and India.

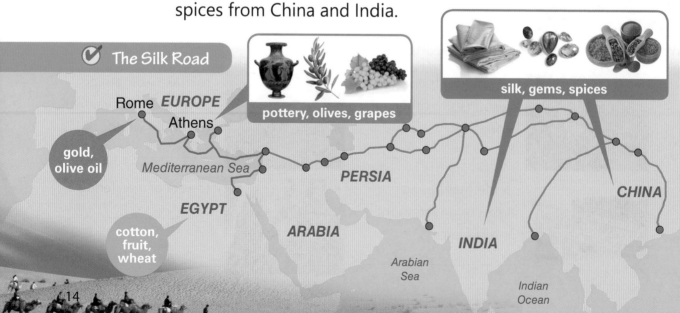

The Silk Road

pottery, olives, grapes

silk, gems, spices

Rome EUROPE
Athens
gold, olive oil
Mediterranean Sea
EGYPT
cotton, fruit, wheat
PERSIA
ARABIA
Arabian Sea
INDIA
CHINA
Indian Ocean

Main Idea and Details

1 **What is the passage mainly about?**

   a. How people conducted trade in the past.

   b. What some items that the Romans traded were.

   c. Which countries the ancient Greeks traded with.

2 **What did the ancient Greeks barter olives for?**

   a. Silk, gems, and spices.   **b.** Cotton, fruit, and wheat.   **c.** Gold and farm goods.

3 **In which region did the ancient Greeks trade with others?**

   a. The Mediterranean Sea.   **b.** China.   **c.** India.

4 **What does benefit mean?**

   a. Invest.   **b.** Try.   **c.** Profit.

5 **Complete the sentences.**

   a. Nowadays, people can trade around the world more _____ than in the past.

   b. The _____ _____ was a route that Roman merchants used to go to China.

   c. The Romans used to trade many goods with people in China and _____.

6 **Complete the outline.**

Ancient Trade

Greeks

- Traded with people around the ᵃ_____ Sea
- Made pottery and grew olives and grapes
- Sailed on ships to Egypt
- Bartered for ᵇ_____, fruit, and wheat

Romans

- Traded with Egypt and other nearby countries
- Traded with ᶜ_____ and India
- Used the Silk Road
- Traded gold and farm goods for silk, ᵈ_____, and spices

Vocabulary Builder

Write the correct word and the meaning in Chinese.

1  ▶ objects that are made out of clay by hand

_____

2  ▶ ancient trade route that extended from eastern China to the Mediterranean Sea

_____

3  ▶ a person who buys or sells goods in large quantities

_____

4  ▶ a powder or seed taken from plants and used to flavor foods

_____

A

Complete the sentences with the words below.

> locator   streams   transportation   rainfall
>
> physical   landforms   territorial   peaks

1   Political maps use lines to show _____ borders, such as state and country borders.

2   A _____ map shows landforms and bodies of water.

3   A road map and a _____ map focus on roads and streets.

4   A _____ map shows where the area of the main map is located.

5   Mountains are high _____ with steep sides.

6   Mt. Everest, the world's highest mountain, and many other high _____ are located in Asia.

7   Rivers are long _____ of water that flow into another body of water.

8   Deserts get very little _____, so most deserts are both hot and arid.

B

Complete the sentences with the words below.

> tariff   benefit   Silk Road   Mediterranean
>
> selling   imported   free market   communication

1   Trade is the buying and _____ of goods and services.

2   Many times, when goods are _____, the buyer must pay a tariff.

3   A _____ is a tax that a government collects on imported goods.

4   In a _____ _____ economy, people decide what to produce and what to buy. _____

5   People trade with each other because they both _____.

6   Thanks to transportation and _____, people around the world can trade more quickly today than ever before.

7   People in ancient Greece used to trade with others around the _____ Sea.

8   Merchants used a route called the _____ _____ to go to China.

C Write the correct word and the meaning in Chinese.

1 ▸ a long row or chain of mountains

_____

2 ▸ the way from one place to another

_____

3 ▸ a smaller map set onto the main map that shows the "big picture" of a place

_____

4 ▸ a ship designed to carry cargo

_____

5 ▸ a group of people who are able to do work

_____

6 ▸ to trade goods without the use of money

_____

D Match each word with the correct definition and write the meaning in Chinese.

1 landform _____ ☐

2 border _____ ☐

3 steep _____ ☐

4 tributary _____ ☐

5 arid _____ ☐

6 export _____ ☐

7 import _____ ☐

8 tariff _____ ☐

9 interference _____ ☐

10 barter _____ ☐

a. very dry

b. the act of interfering

c. a tax on imported goods

d. having a sharp inclination

e. to trade goods without the use of money

f. to sell goods and resources to other countries

g. a stream or river that flows into a larger river

h. to buy goods and resources from other countries

i. a line that divides one state or country from another

j. a different shape of the earth's surface, such as a mountain or desert

05

Key Words

- civilization
- fertile
- topsoil
- silt
- pharaoh
- be descended from
- god-king
- pyramid
- the Sphinx
- temple
- monument
- hieroglyphics

One of the earliest human civilizations formed in Egypt about 5,000 years ago. It was centered on the Nile River. The land around the Nile was very fertile because the river flooded every year. During the floods, the river left rich topsoil and silt on the land. This let farmers grow many crops. Soon, Egypt had a large population.

Ancient Egypt was ruled by pharaohs. They were kings, but people believed the pharaohs were descended from gods. As god-kings, the pharaohs ruled over the Egyptians, who were slaves.

The ancient Egyptians were great engineers and builders. They built enormous pyramids that were tombs for the pharaohs. They also built the Sphinx near the pyramids. And they constructed many other stone temples and monuments throughout the land.

The ancient Egyptians developed a writing system called hieroglyphics. It used pictures and symbols that represented ideas, sound, and objects. Hieroglyphics were carved on walls and monuments.

✔ **The Pyramids and the Sphinx**

the pyramids

the Sphinx

✔ **Egyptian Hieroglyphics**

Main Idea and Details

1 **What is the main idea of the passage?**

   a. The pharaohs were god-kings who ruled over slaves.
   b. The ancient Egyptians built the pyramids.
   c. Ancient Egypt had a very impressive civilization.

2 _____ **were tombs for the pharaohs.**

   a. The Sphinx   **b.** The pyramids   **c.** Hieroglyphics

3 **Why was the land around the Nile very fertile?**

   a. Because the river flooded every year.
   b. Because farmers there grew many crops.
   c. Because the river brought topsoil from the sea.

4 **What does flooded mean?**

   a. Overtook.   **b.** Flowed.   **c.** Overflowed.

5 **According to the passage, which statement is true?**

   a. Ancient Egypt was ruled by gods.   **b.** The Sphinx was carved on walls.
   c. Hieroglyphics formed a picture writing system.

6 **Complete the outline.**

```
                        ┌─────────────────┐
                        │  Ancient Egypt  │
                        └─────────────────┘
```

The Nile River	The Pharaohs	Egyptian Culture
• Was the center of Egyptian civilization • Flooded every year • Left ᵃ_____ land • Helped Egypt have a large ᵇ_____	• Ruled Egypt • Were ᶜ_____ • Ruled over their Egyptian slaves	• Built enormous pyramids, the Sphinx, temples, and monuments • Hieroglyphics = writing system that used pictures and ᵈ_____

Vocabulary Builder

Write the correct word and the meaning in Chinese.

 **1** ▸ a god-king of ancient Egypt

_____

 **2** ▸ a large ancient statue of a creature with a human head and a lion's body that stands near the pyramids in Egypt

_____

 **3** ▸ a large structure that is built to remind people of an event or person

_____

 **4** ▸ a picture writing system used in ancient Egypt

_____

The Culture of Egypt

Key Words

- appearance
- falcon
- jackal
- chaos
- underworld
- fertility
- unite
- conquer
- prosperous
- reign
- preserve
- mummy

The ancient Egyptians worshipped many gods. They often had both human and animal appearances. The most important god was Ra, the sun god. He had a falcon's head. The pharaoh was believed to be a child of Ra. Horus, another god of the sun, had the head of a falcon. Anubis, the god of the dead, had the head of a jackal. Set, or Seth, was the god of chaos. Osiris ruled the underworld. Isis, the sister and wife of Osiris and the mother of Horus, was the goddess of fertility. She also protected people from sickness and harm.

The pharaohs were both wealthy and powerful. Menes became the first pharaoh of Egypt when he united two kingdoms. Ramses II was the greatest and most powerful pharaoh of all. He conquered many lands. Egypt was the most prosperous during the reign of Amenhotep III.

The ancient Egyptians believed they would have new lives after they died. So the culture of Egypt centered on life after death. They developed a way to preserve the dead and could make a body a mummy. Also, Egyptian tombs contained everything a person would need in the next life.

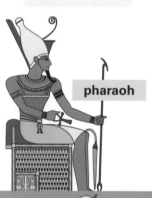

pharaoh

✔ Ancient Egyptian Gods

✔ Mummies

| Ra | Horus | Osiris | Isis | Anubis | Set/Seth |

Main Idea and Details

1   What is the passage mainly about?

a. Some powerful Egyptian gods.   b. Some wealthy and powerful pharaohs.

c. Some features of Egyptian culture.

2   _____ was the most powerful of all Egyptian pharaohs.

a. Amenhotep III   b. Menes   c. Ramses II

3   What was very important in Egyptian culture?

a. Life after death.   b. Life before death.   c. Life before birth.

4   What does prosperous mean?

a. Powerful.   b. Wealthy.   c. Great.

5   Answer the questions.

a. Which Egyptian gods had the head of a falcon? _____

b. Who was the first pharaoh of Egypt? _____

c. What was a mummy? _____

6   Complete the outline.

Egyptian Gods and Pharaohs

Gods	Pharaohs	Life After Death

• Ra = the sun god
• Horus = another god of the sun
• Anubis = the god of the ᵃ_____
• Set/Seth = the god of chaos
• Osiris = the god of the underworld
• Isis = the goddess of ᵇ_____
	• Menes = the first pharaoh
	• ᶜ_____
	  = the greatest pharaoh
	• Amenhotep III
	  = the pharaoh when Egypt
	  was the most prosperous
		• Egyptians believed in life after ᵈ_____.
		• Learned to preserve dead bodies
		• Tombs contained things people needed in their ᵉ_____ _____.

Vocabulary Builder

Write the correct word and the meaning in Chinese.

1 ▸ a wild animal like a dog that lives in Asia and Africa

_____

2 ▸ a state of complete disorder and confusion

_____

3 ▸ the period of time when a king or queen rules a country

_____

4 ▸ a dead body which was wrapped in cloth and preserved long ago

_____

Ancient Greece

Key Words

- brilliant
- city-state
- acropolis
- attack
- enemy
- unite
- birthplace
- democracy
- take part in
- warrior
- defeat
- philosopher
- politician
- general

One of the most brilliant of all ancient civilizations was found in Greece. The Greek people lived in many different city-states. Most city-states were built around an acropolis, a walled hill where people could seek safety from attack. The city-states often fought against each other. But, when foreign enemies like the Persians attacked, they united and fought together.

Athens and Sparta were the two most powerful city-states in ancient Greece. They had different values and cultures.

Athens was the birthplace of democracy. In Athens, citizens were allowed to vote and to take part in the government. But only men could be citizens. The Spartans were tough. They were great warriors. Spartan boys were trained to be soldiers from a young age. Even Spartan girls were trained to compete in sporting events. Athens and Sparta fought the Peloponnesian War against each other. In the end, Sparta defeated Athens.

The Greeks produced many great artists, scientists, philosophers, politicians, and generals. However, in the fourth century B.C., Alexander the Great conquered all of the Greek city-states and united them in his empire.

✔ The Acropolis of Athens

Parthenon

✔ The Collapse of Greek City-States

conquered by Alexander the Great

Main Idea and Details

1 **What is the passage mainly about?**

a. Sparta and Athens.   **b.** The great men produced by ancient Greece.

c. The civilization of ancient Greek city-states.

2 **The birthplace of democracy was _____.**

a. Athens   **b.** Sparta   **c.** Thebes

3 **What was the name of the war that Athens and Sparta fought with each other?**

a. The Persian War.   **b.** The Punic War.   **c.** The Peloponnesian War.

4 **What does take part mean?**

a. Fight.   **b.** Discuss.   **c.** Participate.

5 **Complete the sentences.**

a. The Greek city-states would _____ when there were foreign invaders.

b. Spartan boys were trained to be _____.

c. The Greek city-states were conquered by _____ _____ _____.

6 **Complete the outline.**

Ancient Greece

City-States	Athens	Sparta
• Were built around an acropolis • Often fought against each other • United when ª_____ enemies attacked	• Was the birthplace of ᵇ_____ • Let citizens vote and take part in the ᶜ_____	• Was a warlike society • Defeated Athens during the ᵈ_____ War

Vocabulary Builder

Write the correct word and the meaning in Chinese.

 ▸ a form of government in which people choose leaders by voting

_____

 ▸ a walled hill in ancient Greek cities

_____

 ▸ a person who studies ideas about knowledge, truth, the nature and meaning of life, etc.

_____

 ▸ to win a victory over (someone) in a war

_____

Key Words

- the Socratic Method
- annoy
- custom
- be put on trial
- urge
- revolt
- be sentenced to death
- dialogue
- involve
- ideal
- found

The ancient Greeks produced many great thinkers and philosophers. Greek philosophers studied history, political science, and mathematics. They often taught students as well. The two greatest of all were Socrates and Plato.

Socrates was a teacher in Athens. He led discussions about ways to live. He used a form of questioning called the Socratic Method. Basically, he would ask a series of questions. These questions were designed to find the answer to a problem. Or the questions would show the questioner, such as Socrates, how little he actually knew.

Socrates annoyed many leading Athenians because he began to question the city's laws, customs, and religion. Socrates was put on trial for "urging Athens' young people to revolt." He was found guilty and sentenced to death.

Socrates attracted many students. One of them was named Plato. Plato wrote down all of Socrates' thoughts. He wrote many different books. Most of them were dialogues involving Socrates and other famous Athenians. One of the most famous was the *The Republic*. It described the ideal form of government in Plato's mind. Plato's works became very important and helped found all of Western philosophy.

A law is a law, however undesirable it may be.

✓ **Great Thinkers in Athens**

✓ **The Death of Socrates**

put on trial for misleading young people

sentenced to death by drinking poison

Main Idea and Details

1 **What is the main idea of the passage?**

  a. Socrates created the Socratic Method.

  b. Socrates annoyed many people in ancient Athens.

  c. Socrates and Plato were two great Greek philosophers.

2 **One of the most famous of Plato's works was** _____.

  a. *The Dialogues*　　　　**b.** *The Socratic Method*　　　　**c.** *The Republic*

3 **What happened to Socrates after his trial?**

  a. He was exiled from Athens.

  b. He was sentenced to death.

  c. He was put in jail.

4 **What does urging mean?**

  a. Trying.　　　　**b.** Encouraging.　　　　**c.** Leading.

5 **According to the passage, which statement is true?**

  a. Plato wrote many books as dialogues.

  b. Socrates was the author of *The Republic*.

  c. Socrates was one of Plato's best students.

6 **Complete the outline.**

Greek Philosophers

Socrates

- Led discussions in Athens
- Used the Socratic ᵃ_____
- Asked a ᵇ_____ of questions
- Was put on trial and sentenced to death

Plato

- Was one of Socrates' students
- Wrote many books
- *The Republic* = a book that described the ideal form of ᶜ_____
- Helped found Western ᵈ_____

Vocabulary Builder

Write the correct word and the meaning in Chinese.

 ▸ a legal process in a court to decide whether someone is guilty or not

_____

 ▸ to rebel; to resist

_____

 ▸ to make someone feel slightly angry or impatient

_____

 ▸ to set up; to provide a basis

_____

A Complete the sentences with the words below.

civilizations	tombs	preserve	reign
appearances	writing	descended	died

1 One of the earliest human _____ formed in Egypt about 5,000 years ago.

2 The ancient Egyptians believed the pharaohs were _____ from gods.

3 The ancient Egyptians built enormous pyramids that were _____ for the pharaohs.

4 They developed a _____ system called hieroglyphics.

5 Egyptian gods often had both human and animal _____.

6 Egypt was the most prosperous during the _____ of Amenhotep III.

7 The ancient Egyptians believed they would have new lives after they _____.

8 They developed a way to _____ the dead and could make a body a mummy.

B Complete the sentences with the words below.

questioning	ancient	put on	city-states
philosophers	acropolis	ideal	Peloponnesian

1 One of the most brilliant of all _____ civilizations was found in Greece.

2 Most city-states were built around an _____, a walled hill where people could seek safety from attack.

3 Athens and Sparta were the two most powerful _____ in ancient Greece.

4 Athens and Sparta fought the _____ War against each other.

5 The ancient Greeks produced many great thinkers and _____.

6 Socrates used a form of _____ called the Socratic Method.

7 Socrates was _____ trial for "urging Athens' young people to revolt."

8 *The Republic* described the _____ form of government in Plato's mind.

Write the correct word and the meaning in Chinese.

 1 ▸ a god-king of ancient Egypt

_____

 2 ▸ a picture writing system used in ancient Egypt

_____

 3 ▸ a large bird that is often trained to hunt small animals

_____

 4 ▸ to take control of land or people using soldiers

_____

 5 ▸ a walled hill in ancient Greek cities

_____

 6 ▸ to set up; to provide a basis

_____

D

Match each word with the correct definition and write the meaning in Chinese.

1 temple _____ ☐

2 monument _____ ☐

3 chaos _____ ☐

4 preserve _____ ☐

5 brilliant _____ ☐

6 birthplace _____ ☐

7 defeat _____ ☐

8 revolt _____ ☐

9 ideal _____ ☐

10 found _____ ☐

a. to rebel; to resist

b. to set up; to provide a basis

c. the place where something begins

d. to win a victory over (someone) in a war

e. a state of complete disorder and confusion

f. very bright and sparkling; extremely clever

g. being the best; regarded as perfect of its kind

h. a building used for worship of a god or gods

i. to keep something from being harmed or destroyed

j. a large structure that is built to remind people of an event or person

27

Ancient Rome

Key Words

- peninsula
- Etruscan
- drive out
- republic
- consul
- Senate
- landowner
- patrician
- plebeian
- senator
- Punic Wars
- Carthage
- rival

Early in its history, Rome was a small city located on the Tiber River of the Italian peninsula. As Rome grew, its army conquered many neighboring countries. By 250 B.C., Rome had conquered most of the Italian peninsula.

For 250 years, Rome was ruled by Etruscan kings. In 510 B.C., the Romans drove out the king and founded the Roman Republic. A republic is a form of government in which the government's leaders are elected by the people.

Every year, the wealthy men of the Roman Republic elected two leaders, called consuls. To make decisions on any public plan, both consuls had to agree. The Romans also had a Senate, which advised the consuls. The Senate was a group of wealthy landowners.

There were two classes of citizens in the Roman Republic: patricians and plebeians. The patricians were wealthy men who owned a lot of land. They became consuls and senators. The plebeians were ordinary people. The slaves were the poorest.

In 264 B.C., Rome began the Punic Wars. The Punic Wars were against Carthage, a rival city in Northern Africa. There were three difficult wars, but the Romans finally defeated Carthage in 146 B.C. With its victory, Rome became the world's most powerful empire. It lasted for almost 500 years.

✓ **The Roman Republic**

| The Roman Senate | ◀▶ | 2 consuls |

▲

patricians

▲

plebeians

▲

slaves

✓ **The Punic Wars**

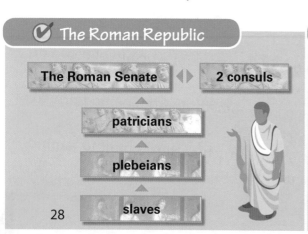

The Carthaginian general Hannibal

Main Idea and Details

1 **What is the passage mainly about?**

    a. Roman patricians and plebeians.

    b. The Roman victory in the Punic Wars.

    c. The rise of the Roman Republic.

2 **The Romans fought the Punic Wars against** _____.

    a. Greece   **b.** Carthage   **c.** Egypt

3 **Who were the two main leaders of the Roman Republic?**

    a. The senators.   **b.** The plebeians.   **c.** The consuls.

4 **What does ordinary mean?**

    a. Regular.   **b.** Wealthy.   **c.** Poor.

5 **Answer the questions.**

    a. Where was Rome located? _____

    b. What happened in 510 B.C.? _____

    c. How many Punic Wars were there? _____

6 **Complete the outline.**

Rome

The Early Years

- Was a small city on the Tiber River
- The ^{a}_____ was founded in 510 B.C.

The System of Government

- ^{b}_____ = leaders of the government
- Senate = landowners who advised the consuls
- Patricians = wealthy landowners
- ^{c}_____ = ordinary people

The Punic Wars

- Were against ^{d}_____
- Were three wars
- Rome defeated Carthage.
- Rome became the world's most powerful ^{e}_____.

Vocabulary Builder

Write the correct word and the meaning in Chinese.

 **1** ▸ a piece of land that is almost completely surrounded by water

_____

 **2** ▸ one of the two elected leaders in charge of ancient Rome

_____

 **3** ▸ a group of landowners who advised the consuls

_____

 **4** ▸ competing

_____

Key Words

- twin
- priestess
- overthrow
- basket
- be thrown into
- float
- rescue
- shepherd
- argue
- name after

Legend says that Rome was founded in 753 B.C. by Romulus and Remus.

Romulus and Remus were twin brothers. The father of these two boys was not a man but Mars, the Roman god of war. And their mother was the priestess Rhea Silvia. Their grandfather once was a king but had been overthrown.

When Romulus and Remus were born, they were put into a basket and thrown into the Tiber River. The new king, Amulius, feared that someday the boys might overthrow him.

Luckily, the basket floated to the edge of the river, and the boys were rescued by a mother wolf. She took care of the babies as if they were her own. Later, a shepherd took the boys and raised them.

When the boys grew up, they learned about their history. They killed Amulius and made their grandfather king again.

Romulus and Remus decided to build their own city. But they argued over many things. During one terrible argument, Romulus killed Remus. Romulus finished building his city on the seven hills on the Tiber River. He named the city Rome after himself.

 Romulus and Remus　　 Ruins of Ancient Rome

nursed by the wolf that rescued them

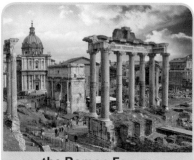

the Roman Forum

the Colosseum

Main Idea and Details

1 **What is the passage mainly about?**

   a. The history of Rome.

   b. The killing of Amulius.

   c. The story of Romulus and Remus.

2 **Romulus and Remus were rescued from the river by a _____.**

   a. shepherd   **b.** king   **c.** wolf

3 **Who was the father of Romulus and Remus?**

   a. The god Mars.   **b.** Amulius.   **c.** A shepherd.

4 **What does rescued mean?**

   a. Saved.   **b.** Seen.   **c.** Raised.

5 **Complete the sentences.**

   a. The mother of Romulus and Remus was the priestess _____ _____.

   b. A _____ raised Romulus and Remus.

   c. _____ killed Remus while they had an argument.

6 **Complete the outline.**

Romulus and Remus

Their Parents	Their Lives	The Founding of Rome
• Father was the god ᵃ _____. • Mother was the priestess Rhea Silvia.	• Were thrown into the ᵇ _____ _____ • Were rescued by a mother wolf • Were ᶜ _____ by a shepherd • Killed Amulius and made their grandfather king again	• Decided to build their own city • Romulus killed Remus during an ᵈ _____. • Romulus finished building his city and called it ᵉ _____.

Vocabulary Builder

Write the correct word and the meaning in Chinese.

1  ► a female priest in non-Christian religions

_____

2  ► to remove a leader or government from power by force

_____

3  ► to be carried along by moving water

_____

4  ► to save someone from a dangerous or unpleasant situation

_____

Key Words

- collapse
- split
- invader
- Middle Ages
- die of
- hunger
- disease
- official
- expand
- reunite
- troops

The Roman Empire collapsed in 476. The Romans had controlled all the land along the coast of the Mediterranean Sea and in most parts of Europe. By the 300s and 400s, the Roman Empire had grown too big for one man to rule, so it was split in two: the Western Roman Empire and the Eastern Roman Empire.

The Western Roman Empire was conquered by Germanic invaders in 476. But the Eastern Roman Empire, also known as the Byzantine Empire, lasted until 1453. We call the period between the fall of Western Roman Empire and the 1400s the Middle Ages.

The early Middle Ages are often called "the Dark Ages" because few Europeans could read or write. For most Europeans, life during this time was hard and dangerous. Many people died of war, hunger, and disease.

However, for the Christian Church, the Middle Ages were a time of growth. Christianity became the official religion of the Roman Empire under Emperor Constantine in 313, and it continued to expand even after the Western Roman Empire fell. By the year 800, Charlemagne reunited much of Western Europe and spread Christianity wherever his troops went. Eventually, the church grew wealthy and powerful.

✔ *Christianity expanded during the Middle Ages.*

Emperor Constantine

made Christianity the official religion

Charlemagne, Charles the Great

spread Christianity all over Western Europe

Main Idea and Details

1   What is the passage mainly about?

a. The Middle Ages and the Church.   **b.** The fall of the Roman Empire.

c. The Christian Church.

2   The Eastern Roman Empire was called the _____.

a. Christian Empire   **b.** Holy Roman Empire   **c.** Byzantine Empire

3   Who reunited much of Western Europe by the year 800?

a. Constantine.   **b.** Charlemagne.   **c.** Julius Caesar.

4   What does collapsed mean?

a. Divided.   **b.** Conquered.   **c.** Fell.

5   According to the passage, which statement is true?

a. Charlemagne became the ruler of the Byzantine Empire in 800.

b. Germanic invaders conquered the Western Roman Empire in 476.

c. Christianity did not spread very much during the Middle Ages.

6   Complete the outline.

The Middle Ages

The Roman Empire	The Dark Ages	The Christian Church
• Was divided into eastern and a_____ parts • The Western Rome Empire was conquered by b_____ invaders in 476.	• Was the early Middle Ages • Few Europeans could read or write then. • People died of war, c_____, and disease.	• Grew during the Middle Ages • Became the official religion under d_____ _____ in 313

Vocabulary Builder

Write the correct word and the meaning in Chinese.

 **1**   ► to divide

_____

 **2**   ► a person or group that invades a country, region, or other place

_____

 **3**   ► to become larger in size and fill more space

_____

 **4**   ► organized groups of soldiers

_____

12

Key Words

- feudalism
- practice
- fief
- lord
- vassal
- swear
- oath
- knight
- loyalty
- metal armor
- horseback
- feudal
- serf
- manor

During the Middle Ages, a unique social system called feudalism arose. It was mostly practiced in England, France, and Germany.

In feudalism, land was exchanged for service. In many places, kings divided their land into fiefs. Fiefs were large areas of land controlled by the local lords. A lord divided his fief among his vassals. The vassals received smaller fiefs of their own. The vassals were supposed to keep their fiefs only as long as they faithfully served their king or lord. Vassals, lords, and kings swore oaths to keep these rules.

One way a vassal served his lord or king was by providing knights when they were needed. Knights swore loyalty to their lord and their king. In battle, they wore metal armor and often fought on horseback.

At the bottom of feudal society were the small farmers called serfs, or peasants. Serfs had few rights. They had to work on the manors owned by the lords. They could not move away from a manor without the lord's permission.

✔ Life in the Middle Ages

manor / manor house

Lords lived in manors and managed large areas of land.

Serfs were poor and had to work on their lords' manors.

The vassals were supposed to keep their fiefs only as long as they faithfully served their king or lord.

Knights were loyal to their lord and their king.

Main Idea and Details

1 **What is the passage mainly about?**

a. How feudalism was founded.

b. How feudalism worked.

c. How feudalism benefitted everyone.

2 **Lords lived in _____ that they owned.**

a. vassals   **b.** serfs   **c.** manors

3 **What did vassals provide for their lord or king?**

a. Manors.   **b.** Knights.   **c.** Fiefs.

4 **What does faithfully mean?**

a. Loyally.   **b.** Constantly.   **c.** Occasionally.

5 **Complete the sentences.**

a. A large area of land that a lord controlled was called a _____.

b. Vassals swore _____ of loyalty to their lords.

c. _____ were farmers with few rights in feudalism.

6 **Complete the outline.**

Feudalism

How It Worked	What Vassals Did	Serfs
• Kings gave fiefs to ᵃ_____. • A lord divided his fief among his ᵇ_____.	• Faithfully served their lord or king • Provided ᶜ_____ when their lord or king needed them	• Were poor farmers or peasants • Had few rights • Worked on ᵈ_____ owned by lords

Vocabulary Builder

Write the correct word and the meaning in Chinese.

1  ▸ a social system in the Middle Ages

_____

2  ▸ to make a very serious promise

_____

3  ▸ someone who lived and worked on land belonging to another person

_____

4  ▸ a large house with a lot of land and small buildings around it; the main house on such an area of land

_____

Vocabulary Review 3

A Complete the sentences with the words below.

Tiber River	Carthage	Italian	thrown
consuls	founded	republic	grew up

1 Early in its history, Rome was a small city located on the Tiber River of the _____ peninsula.

2 A _____ is a form of government in which the government's leaders are elected by the people.

3 Every year, the wealthy men of the Roman Republic elected two leaders, called _____.

4 The Punic Wars were against _____, a rival city in Northern Africa.

5 Legend says that Rome was _____ in 753 B.C. by Romulus and Remus.

6 When Romulus and Remus were born, they were put into a basket and _____ into the Tiber River.

7 When the boys _____ _____, they learned about their history.

8 Romulus finished building his city on the seven hills on the _____ _____.

B Complete the sentences with the words below.

feudalism	Western	Dark Ages	peasants
Christianity	fiefs	wealthy	loyalty

1 The Roman Empire was split in two: the _____ Roman Empire and the Eastern Roman Empire.

2 The early Middle Ages are often called "the _____ _____."

3 _____ became the official religion of the Roman Empire under Emperor Constantine in 313.

4 Eventually, the church grew _____ and powerful.

5 During the Middle Ages, a unique social system called _____ arose.

6 _____ were large areas of land controlled by the local lords.

7 Knights swore _____ to their lord and their king.

8 At the bottom of feudal society were the small farmers called serfs, or _____.

C Write the correct word and the meaning in Chinese.

1 ▸ a piece of land that is almost completely surrounded by water

_____

2 ▸ a group of landowners who advised the consuls

_____

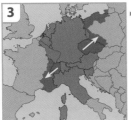
3 ▸ to become larger in size and fill more space

_____

4 ▸ someone whose job is to take care of sheep

_____

5 ▸ a man who fought in battle for his king or lord in the Middle Ages

_____

6 ▸ a person in the past who received protection and land from a lord in return for loyalty and service

_____

D Match each word with the correct definition and write the meaning in Chinese.

1 patrician _____ ☐

2 drive out _____ ☐

3 overthrow _____ ☐

4 argue _____ ☐

5 split _____ ☐

6 invaders _____ ☐

7 official _____ ☐

8 feudalism _____ ☐

9 swear _____ ☐

10 armor _____ ☐

a. to divide
b. to kick out; to expel
c. to quarrel; to dispute
d. a wealthy landowner
e. to make a very serious promise
f. a social system in the Middle Ages
g. soldiers who are invading a country
h. to remove a leader or government from power by force
i. metal or leather clothing worn by men in battle in past times
j. approved by the government or by someone in authority

Wrap-Up Test 1

A

Write the correct word for each sentence.

thinkers	service	empty	brilliant	Egyptians
imported	merchants	preserve	borders	Middle Ages

1 Political maps use lines to show territorial _____, such as state and country borders.

2 Many tributaries _____ into large rivers.

3 A tariff is a tax that a government collects on _____ goods.

4 _____ used a route called the Silk Road to go to China.

5 The ancient _____ were great engineers and builders.

6 The ancient Egyptians developed a way to _____ the dead and could make a body a mummy.

7 One of the most _____ of all ancient civilizations was found in Greece.

8 The ancient Greeks produced many great _____ and philosophers.

9 In feudalism, land was exchanged for _____.

10 For the Christian Church, the _____ _____ were a time of growth.

B

Write the meanings of the words in Chinese.

1	mountain range	_____	16 monument	_____
2	route	_____	17 chaos	_____
3	locator	_____	18 preserve	_____
4	cargo ship	_____	19 brilliant	_____
5	merchant	_____	20 revolt	_____
6	spice	_____	21 peninsula	_____
7	landform	_____	22 the Senate	_____
8	border	_____	23 priestess	_____
9	steep	_____	24 shepherd	_____
10	tributary	_____	25 knight	_____
11	arid	_____	26 patrician	_____
12	tariff	_____	27 overthrow	_____
13	interference	_____	28 vassal	_____
14	hieroglyphics	_____	29 fief	_____
15	mummy	_____	30 feudalism	_____

2

Science

Key Words

- inquiry
- scientific method
- figure out
- observation
- hypothesis
- prediction
- testable
- conduct
- interpret
- draw a conclusion

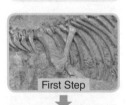

First Step

Second Step

Third Step

Fourth Step

Fifth Step

Do you sometimes ask "why" questions when you are curious about the things around you? Scientists often ask questions about things in our world, too. When scientists want to answer a question, they use inquiry skills called the scientific method. The scientific method is a way that scientists use to solve a problem and to figure out how things work.

Scientists often use the following five steps in the scientific method.

❶ Observation and Question

Scientists observe things carefully and ask a question. Asking and answering questions is the basis of inquiry.

❷ Hypothesis

Scientists make a prediction based on what they observe. A good hypothesis must be testable with an experiment.

❸ Experiment

The third step is to conduct experiments. Experiments are very important for testing the hypothesis.

❹ Collecting and Interpreting Data

Collecting and interpreting data are the essential parts of an experiment. Scientists often use math skills when they collect and interpret data.

❺ Conclusion

Now, it is time to draw a conclusion. Do the results support the hypothesis or not? If the hypothesis was not correct, scientists form another hypothesis and test it again.

Main Idea and Details

1   What is the main idea of the passage?
   a. There are five steps in the scientific method.
   b. Scientists need to observe the world around them.
   c. Most scientists ask questions to solve problems.

2   The third step in the scientific method is to _____.
   a. collect data   **b.** make predictions   **c.** conduct experiments

3   What is a good hypothesis?
   a. One that asks questions.   **b.** One that provides a good conclusion.
   c. One that can be tested with an experiment.

4   What does make a prediction mean?
   a. Inquire.   **b.** Predict.   **c.** Conclude.

5   Complete the sentences.
   a. The basis of _____ is asking and answering questions.
   b. A scientist tests a _____ by conducting experiments.
   c. The last step in the scientific method is to draw a _____.

6   Complete the outline.

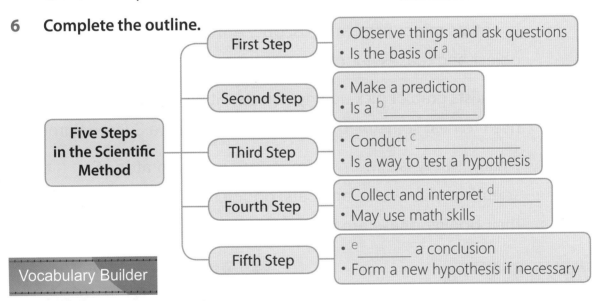

Five Steps in the Scientific Method

First Step
- Observe things and ask questions
- Is the basis of [a]_____

Second Step
- Make a prediction
- Is a [b]_____

Third Step
- Conduct [c]_____
- Is a way to test a hypothesis

Fourth Step
- Collect and interpret [d]_____
- May use math skills

Fifth Step
- [e]_____ a conclusion
- Form a new hypothesis if necessary

Vocabulary Builder

Write the correct word and the meaning in Chinese.

 **1** ▸ the process of watching someone or something carefully, in order to find something out

_____

 **2** ▸ a prediction based on what a scientist has observed

_____

 **3** ▸ to explain the meaning of something; to understand something in a specified way

_____

 **4** ▸ to conclude

_____

41

14

Key Words

- laboratory = lab
- instrument
- observe
- manipulate
- volume
- beaker
- graduated cylinder
- hand lens
- magnifying glass
- microscope
- magnify
- forceps

Scientists do much work in laboratories. These labs are often filled with all kinds of scientific tools and instruments. Scientists use tools to measure, observe, and manipulate things.

To find the volume of a liquid, scientists use a measuring cup, a beaker, or a graduated cylinder. A thermometer measures temperature, a scale measures weight, and a ruler measures length.

Sometimes scientists need to observe an object closely. When they want to observe details, they might use a hand lens or a magnifying glass. These are small, handheld instruments that make objects appear larger than they really are. For very small objects, scientists might use a microscope. A microscope magnifies an object and makes it look several times bigger than it is.

Scientists grab or pick up tiny objects with forceps. And, when they need to heat something, they will probably use a Bunsen burner.

Finally, safety is extremely important in a laboratory. So, scientists often wear lab coats, goggles, and gloves to protect their bodies. These are important tools, too.

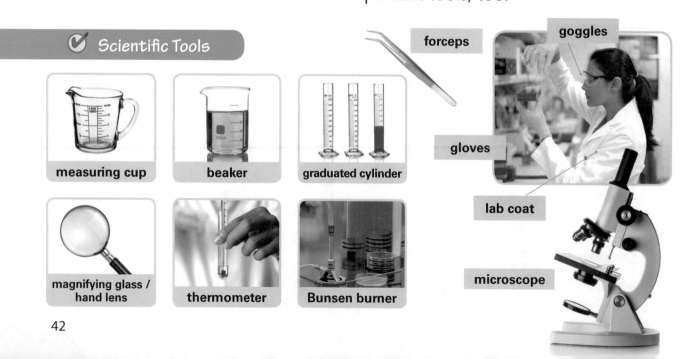

Scientific Tools

measuring cup

beaker

graduated cylinder

forceps

goggles

gloves

lab coat

microscope

magnifying glass / hand lens

thermometer

Bunsen burner

Main Idea and Details

1 **What is the passage mainly about?**

a. What safety equipment scientists wear.   **b.** How to measure different substances.

c. The equipment found in scientific laboratories.

2 **Scientists can measure weight with a _____.**

a. thermometer   **b.** ruler   **c.** scale

3 **What do scientists use to grab tiny objects?**

a. Forceps.   **b.** Goggles.   **c.** A microscope.

4 **What does observe mean?**

a. Look for.   **b.** Look at.   **c.** Look to.

5 **According to the passage, which statement is true?**

a. Lab coats help protect people's bodies.

b. Microscopes can make objects appear tiny.

c. A beaker can measure the length of an object.

6 **Complete the outline.**

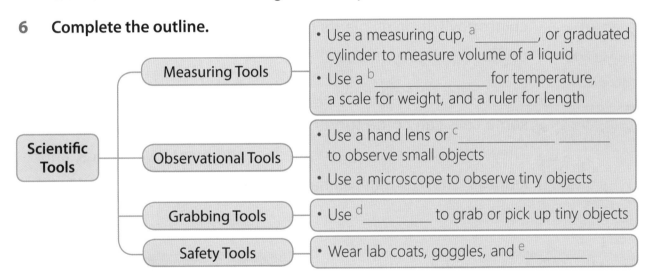

Scientific Tools

Measuring Tools
- Use a measuring cup, ^a_____, or graduated cylinder to measure volume of a liquid
- Use a ^b_____ for temperature, a scale for weight, and a ruler for length

Observational Tools
- Use a hand lens or ^c_____ _____ to observe small objects
- Use a microscope to observe tiny objects

Grabbing Tools
- Use ^d_____ to grab or pick up tiny objects

Safety Tools
- Wear lab coats, goggles, and ^e_____

Vocabulary Builder

Write the correct word and the meaning in Chinese.

 **1**
▸ a room or building where a scientist does experiments or research

_____

 **2**
▸ to handle something or to work it with the hands in a skillful way

_____

 **3**
▸ a glass or plastic container with straight sides that is used in a laboratory

_____

 **4**
▸ a tool that is used for grasping or holding things

_____

🎧 15

Key Words

- cell
- unit
- organism
- nucleus
- cell membrane
- cytoplasm
- cell wall
- stiff
- chloroplast
- chlorophyll
- photosynthesis
- specialized
- tissue
- organ

Cells are the basic units of life. All living things are made of cells. Big or small, every organism is made of at least one or more cells.

Plant and animal cells have many of the same parts. All cells have a nucleus, the control center of the cell. The outer covering of a cell is the cell membrane. And both plant and animal cells are filled with cytoplasm.

But plant cells differ in some ways. Plant cells have cell walls, which is the stiff layer outside the cell membrane. Another important part of plants is chloroplasts. Chloroplasts contain chlorophyll. It gives plants their green color and lets them undergo photosynthesis.

Many animals' cells have specialized purposes. For instance, some cells can come together to form tissues such as muscles. They can also create organs such as the heart, liver, lungs, and kidneys. These organs all have important roles in animals' bodies.

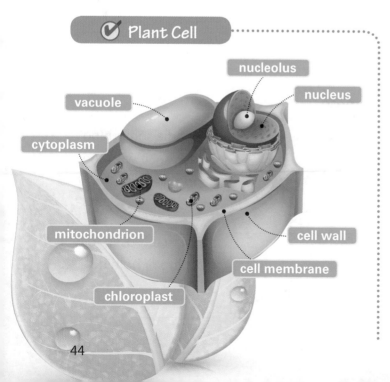

✔ Plant Cell

nucleolus

nucleus

vacuole

cytoplasm

mitochondrion

cell wall

cell membrane

chloroplast

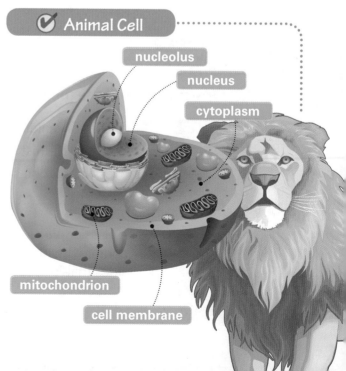

✔ Animal Cell

nucleolus

nucleus

cytoplasm

mitochondrion

cell membrane

Main Idea and Details

1 **What is the main idea of the passage?**

  a. Plant and animal cells are not entirely the same.

  b. Cells are the most important parts of plants and animals.

  c. The important organs in the body are made of cells.

2 **Plant cells have _____, but animal cells do not.**

  a. a nucleus   **b.** cell walls   **c.** a cell membrane

3 **Where is chlorophyll found?**

  a. In the cell wall.   **b.** In organs.   **c.** In chloroplasts.

4 **What does stiff mean?**

  a. Rigid.   **b.** Powerful.   **c.** Green.

5 **Answer the questions.**

  a. What do all plant and animal cells have?

  _____

  b. What do plant cells have that animal cells do not? _____

  c. What are some specialized purposes of cells? _____

6 **Complete the outline.**

Plant and Animal Cells

Similarities	Differences	Specialized Roles of Animal Cells
• Nucleus = control part of a cell • a _____ _____ = outer covering • Cytoplasm = filling in cells	• Plant cells have cell walls. • Plant cells have chloroplasts, which contains b _____.	• Can form c _____ such as muscles • Can create d _____ such as the heart, liver, lungs, and kidneys

Vocabulary Builder

Write the correct word and the meaning in Chinese.

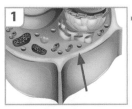 ▸ a very thin layer that surrounds the cytoplasm of a cell

_____

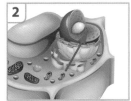 ▸ the control part of a cell

_____

 ▸ a part of plants that contains chlorophyll

_____

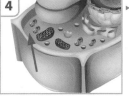 ▸ the substance inside the cells of living things, not including the nucleus

_____

Classifying Living Things

Key Words

- billion
- in common
- one-celled
- multi-celled
- microorganism
- microscopic organism
- bacterium (*pl.* bacteria)
- virus
- protist
- fungus (*pl.* fungi)

There are millions of types of animals and plants on Earth. The basic unit of all organisms is the cell. Some organisms are only formed of one cell while others, like humans, are made up of billions of different cells.

Organisms are grouped by features they have in common. One way to classify organisms is the cells. Scientists often compare one-celled organisms to multi-celled organisms.

The smallest organisms on Earth are microorganisms, or microscopic organisms. They are so small that a person cannot see them without using a microscope. Many microorganisms are one-celled organisms. Bacteria, viruses, and protists are three different types of microorganisms. They have everything that they need to live in a single cell.

Most organisms have more than one cell. We call them multi-celled organisms. Reptiles, fish, amphibians, mammals, and birds are all multi-celled organisms. Fungi and plants are also multi-celled organisms.

Classification of Organisms

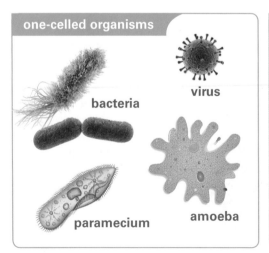

one-celled organisms

bacteria

virus

paramecium

amoeba

multi-celled organisms

Main Idea and Details

1 What is the main idea of the passage?

a. Organisms can be grouped by cells.

b. There are different types of multi-celled organisms.

c. Bacteria, viruses, and protists are one-celled organisms.

2 Bacteria and viruses are types of _____.

a. multi-celled organisms   b. protists   c. microorganisms

3 How are living things classified?

a. By using a microscope.   b. By what they need to live.

c. By characteristics they have in common.

4 What does grouped mean?

a. Split.   b. Classified.   c. Reproduced.

5 Complete the sentences.

a. Organisms can be made of one _____ or billions of them.

b. _____ are the smallest types of organisms.

c. _____ organisms include mammals, reptiles, and birds.

6 Complete the outline.

> Classifying Organisms

> One-Celled Organisms

> Multi-Celled Organisms

- Many ᵃ_____ have one cell.
- Include bacteria, ᵇ_____, and protists

- Most organisms have more than one cell.
- Include animals, like ᶜ_____, fish, amphibians, mammals, and birds
- Include ᵈ_____ and plants

Vocabulary Builder

Write the correct word and the meaning in Chinese.

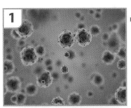 ► extremely small; seen only through a microscope

_____

 ► very small organisms, some can cause disease, but some are good for health

_____

 ► a type of plant without leaves, flowers, or green color that grows mainly in wet places or on decaying substances

_____

 ► having many cells

_____

Vocabulary **Review 4**

A

Complete the sentences with the words below.

> scientific method   laboratory   magnifies   inquiry
> interpreting   hypothesis   forceps   manipulate

1 When scientists want to answer a question, they use inquiry skills called the
_____ _____.

2 Asking and answering questions is the basis of _____.

3 A good _____ must be testable with an experiment.

4 Collecting and _____ data are the essential parts of an experiment.

5 Scientists use tools to measure, observe, and _____ things.

6 A microscope _____ an object and makes it look several times bigger
than it is.

7 Scientists grab or pick up tiny objects with _____.

8 Safety is extremely important in a _____.

B

Complete the sentences with the words below.

> photosynthesis   organism   nucleus   features
> multi-celled   protists   tissues   cell walls

1 Big or small, every _____ is made of at least one or more cell.

2 All cells have a _____, the control center of the cell.

3 Plant cells have _____ _____, which is the stiff layer outside the cell
membrane.

4 Chlorophyll gives plants their green color and lets them undergo
_____.

5 Some cells can come together to form _____ such as muscles.

6 Organisms are grouped by _____ they have in common.

7 Scientists often compare one-celled organisms to _____ organisms.

8 Bacteria, viruses, and _____ are three different types of microorganisms.

C

Write the correct word and the meaning in Chinese.

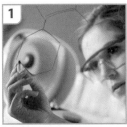
1 ► to conclude

_____

2 ► a tool that makes tiny objects look bigger

_____

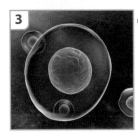
3 ► the basic unit of all life

_____

4 ► any organism, such as bacteria, of microscopic size

_____

5 ► a part of plants that contains chlorophyll

_____

6 ► to make something appear larger

_____

D

Match each word with the correct definition and write the meaning in Chinese.

1 inquiry _____ ☐

2 hypothesis _____ ☐

3 figure out _____ ☐

4 draw a conclusion _____ ☐

5 manipulate _____ ☐

6 nucleus _____ ☐

7 specialized _____ ☐

8 microorganism _____ ☐

9 one-celled _____ ☐

10 multi-celled _____ ☐

a. to conclude

b. having a single cell

c. having many cells

d. the control part of a cell

e. to understand; to calculate

f. developed for a particular purpose

g. any organism, such as bacteria, of microscopic size

h. the process of asking and answering questions; a question

i. a prediction based on what a scientist has observed

j. to handle something or to work it with the hands in a skillful way

What Is Heredity?

Key Words

- similarity
- heredity
- pass down
- trait
- offspring
- gene
- sperm
- genetic material
- inherit
- dominant gene
- recessive gene
- determine

Have you ever wondered why you look like your parents? Perhaps you have the same eye color as your father. Or perhaps you and your mother have similar-looking noses. The reason for these similarities is heredity. Heredity is the passing down of certain traits from parents to their offspring.

The basic unit of heredity is the gene. Genes carry instructions for how an organism will grow and develop. Every human has the same number of genes, but the instructions on the genes vary. That is why every human has different traits.

Genes are transferred from parents to offspring when a sperm cell and an egg cell join. This means half of the genetic material comes from the mother, and half comes from the father. So the children will inherit the traits of both of their parents.

However, there are two types of genes. They are dominant and recessive genes. Dominant genes are stronger than recessive genes. Recessive genes are in the body, but they do not do anything. Dominant genes are the ones that actually determine an organism's traits and appearance.

✓ *Organisms pass on genetic material to their offspring.*

Main Idea and Details

1 **What is the passage mainly about?**

a. The definition of heredity.   **b.** Dominant and recessive genes.

c. Genes and how they are transferred.

2 **The _____ is the basic unit of heredity.**

a. sperm   **b.** egg   **c.** gene

3 **Which genes determine an organism's traits and appearance?**

a. Dominant genes.   **b.** Recessive genes.

c. Dominant and recessive genes.

4 **What does passing down mean?**

a. Throwing.   **b.** Transferring.   **c.** Moving.

5 **According to the passage, which statement is true?**

a. Offspring pass their genes on to their parents.

b. Humans have the same number of genes.

c. Recessive genes are stronger than dominant genes.

6 **Complete the outline.**

Heredity

Genes	Transferring Genes	Dominant and Recessive Genes
• Are the basic units of heredity • Carry a_____ for how organisms will grow and develop	• Happens when a sperm cell and an b_____ _____ join • Half of the genetic material comes from the father and half from the mother.	• Dominant genes = determine an organism's c_____ and appearance • d_____ genes = are in the body but do not do anything

Vocabulary Builder

Write the correct word and the meaning in Chinese.

 **1** ▸ the passing down of traits from parents to their offspring

_____

 **2** ▸ the basic unit of heredity

_____

 **3** ▸ a person's child or an animal's young

_____

4 ▸ the quality or state of being similar

_____

What Are Traits?

 18

Key Words

- trait
- characteristic
- affect
- combination
- nurture
- inherited trait
- learned trait
- spot
- alter
- influence

A trait is a particular characteristic that organisms have. All organisms have different traits. Some traits are affected only by genes. However, some traits develop through a combination of genes and nurture. We can divide the traits into two groups: inherited traits and learned traits.

Inherited traits are characteristics that come from your parents. For humans, eye color, hair color, and the shape of the nose are all inherited traits. The great size of elephants and the spots of leopards are other inherited traits. Organisms cannot alter their inherited traits. These traits are determined only by the genes passed down from their parents.

However, learned traits are different. Nurturing and the environment can influence many traits. You cannot change your eye color, but you can change some characteristics by the way you live. For instance, you might change your height. If you eat healthy food and exercise, your body can grow taller than your gene's information. Knowing how to read and how to ride a bicycle are also learned traits.

☑ Humans have two kinds of traits.

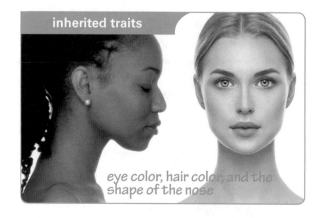

inherited traits

eye color, hair color, and the shape of the nose

learned traits

height and knowing how to read

Main Idea and Details

1   **What is the main idea of the passage?**

a. Genes affect most of the traits people have.

b. There are both inherited traits and learned traits.

c. Nurturing has an effect on people's traits.

2   **Nurturing and _____ can affect a person's learned traits.**

a. genes   b. the environment   c. inherited traits

3   **Which trait is affected by nurture?**

a. Eye color.   b. Spots of leopards.   c. Height.

4   **What does alter mean?**

a. Develop.   b. Nurture.   c. Change.

5   **Answer the questions.**

a. What is a trait? _____

b. What are some inherited traits that humans have?

_____

c. Where do inherited traits come from? _____

6   **Complete the outline.**

```
                            Traits
         ┌──────────────────┴──────────────────┐
   Inherited Traits                      Learned Traits
```

• Come from one's ᵃ_____
• Include eye color, hair color, and the shape of one's nose
• Cannot be altered
• Are determined by ᵇ_____

• Are influenced by nurturing and the ᶜ_____
• Can be affected by the way a person lives
• Include ᵈ_____ and knowing how to read and how to ride a bicycle

Vocabulary Builder

Write the correct word and the meaning in Chinese.

 **1** ▸ a particular characteristic that organisms have

_____

 **2** ▸ a characteristics that come from one's parents

_____

 **3** ▸ a behavior that results from the influence of one's environment

_____

 **4** ▸ care, nourishment, and encouragement given to a growing child

_____

The Formation of the Earth

Key Words

- geologic time scale
- era
- Precambrian Era
- comprise
- Paleozoic Era
- stabilize
- evolve
- Mesozoic Era
- dominate
- Cenozoic Era
- refer to . . . as . . .

Around 4.5 billion years ago, the earth formed. During that time, the planet has undergone many changes. Scientists have divided the history of the earth into different time periods. This is called the geologic time scale. The geologic time scale is divided into several eras. Each era is an extremely long period of time.

The Precambrian Era was the first. It comprised about 90% of all the earth's history. It covered the time from Earth's creation to about 600 million years ago. During this time, the earth was still extremely hot since it was just forming. Also, the earth's atmosphere began to gain oxygen, and plants and animals started to develop.

Next was the Paleozoic Era. It lasted for around 300 million years. Earth's oxygen level stabilized. Invertebrates, fish, and reptiles evolved during it.

The Mesozoic Era lasted for around 150 million years. This era is often known as the age of the dinosaurs. Dinosaurs dominated this period, but small mammals began to evolve.

Today, we live in the Cenozoic Era. It has lasted for about 65 million years. Scientists often refer to it as the time of mammals.

The Geologic Time Scale

Precambrian Era	Paleozoic Era	Mesozoic Era	Cenozoic Era

trilobite

ammonite

mammoth

One-celled organisms were dominant. **Trilobites were dominant.** **Dinosaurs were dominant.** **Humans first appeared.**

Main Idea and Details

1 **What is the main idea of the passage?**
   a. The earth was created about 4.5 billion years ago.
   b. The current era on the planet is the Cenozoic Era.
   c. There have been several eras in the earth's development.

2 **Invertebrates, fish, and reptiles began to evolve during the _____.**
   a. Cenozoic Era   **b.** Mesozoic Era   **c.** Paleozoic Era

3 **What happened during the Precambrian Era?**
   a. Plants and animals began to develop.   **b.** The dinosaurs began to evolve.
   c. Humans and other mammals dominated.

4 **What does comprised mean?**
   a. Occurred.   **b.** Covered.   **c.** Discussed.

5 **Complete the sentences.**
   a. The earth's atmosphere began to gain _____ in the Precambrian Era.
   b. The _____ _____ lasted for around 300 million years.
   c. Small mammals began to evolve during the _____ _____.

6 **Complete the outline.**

The Earth's Eras

Precambrian Era
- Comprised 90% of the earth's history
- Atmosphere began to gain ª_____.
- Plants and animals started to develop.

Paleozoic Era
- Lasted for 300 million years
- The oxygen level stabilized.
- Invertebrates, fish, and ᵇ_____ evolved.

Mesozoic Era
- Was the age of ᶜ_____
- Lasted for 150 million years
- Small mammals began to evolve.

Cenozoic Era
- Is the ᵈ_____ era
- Has lasted for 65 million years

Vocabulary Builder

Write the correct word and the meaning in Chinese.

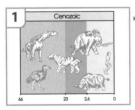 1 ▸ a system of chronological dating that relates geological strata to time

_____

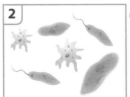 2 ▸ the earliest era of geological history

_____

 3 ▸ to develop by gradually changing or to make something do this

_____

 4 ▸ to have power and control over someone or something

_____

Key Words

- **supercontinent**
- **Pangaea**
- **assume**
- **pull apart**
- **mystery**
- **theory**
- **continental drift**
- **crust**
- **plate**
- **mantle**
- **melted rock**

Today, there are seven continents on the earth. But the earth's surface did not always look this way. Scientists believe that millions of years ago, there was just one supercontinent on the entire Earth. It was called Pangaea. Scientists also assume that the continents joined together and then pulled apart at several times in the earth's history.

How did it happen? The mystery is explained by a theory of continental drift. The theory explains that Earth's continents move very slowly from one position to another.

The continents are all on the earth's crust. There are many huge plates that make up the crust. The crust is solid. However, beneath it is the mantle. Much of the mantle is hot, melted rock which can flow like a liquid. This melted rock moves the crust above it. So the plates are constantly in motion. Even today, the continents move a few millimeters every year.

As a result, the earth's surface is continually changing. If these changes continue, the earth's surface will look very different in another million years.

The Theory of Continental Drift

Pangaea, the supercontinent, formed millions of years ago.

Gradually, Pangaea broke up into several pieces.

Main Idea and Details

1 **What is the passage mainly about?**

a. How the earth's continents move and change.

b. Why Pangaea does not exist today.

c. Where Pangaea used to be located.

2 **The supercontinent that used to be on Earth is called _____.**

a. Continental drift   b. Pangaea   c. Crust

3 **What makes the crust move?**

a. Pangaea.   b. Melted rock.   c. Solids.

4 **What does constantly mean?**

a. Seldom.   b. Frequently.   c. Always.

5 **According to the passage, which statement is true?**

a. Pangaea is the name of the largest continent on the earth today.

b. There are huge plates that make up the earth's crust.

c. Scientists believe Pangaea will form again in a million years.

6 **Complete the outline.**

Continental Drift

Pangaea

- Was a ᵃ_____ that existed millions of years ago
- ᵇ_____ apart when the surface of the earth changed

How It Works

- There are huge plates on the ᶜ_____.
- The crust sits on top of the mantle, much of which is melted rock.
- The ᵈ_____ _____ keeps the plates in constant motion.

Vocabulary Builder

Write the correct word and the meaning in Chinese.

 ▸ a great landmass that was called Pangaea

_____

 ▸ the gradual movement and formation of continents

_____

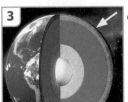 ▸ a large piece of the earth's surface that makes up the crust

_____

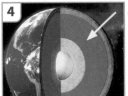 ▸ the earth's thickest layer, which is comprised of melted rock

_____

A

Complete the sentences with the words below.

> information   genes   inherited   influence
> characteristic   dominant   recessive   passing down

1 Heredity is the _____ _____ of certain traits from parents to their offspring.

2 _____ carry instructions for how an organism will grow and develop.

3 _____ genes are the ones that actually determine an organism's traits and appearance.

4 _____ genes are in the body, but they do not do anything.

5 A trait is a particular _____ that organisms have.

6 _____ traits are characteristics that come from your parents.

7 Nurturing and the environment can _____ many traits.

8 If you eat healthy food and exercise, your body can grow taller than your gene's _____.

B

Complete the sentences with the words below.

> melted rock   supercontinent   Paleozoic   Precambrian
> time periods   dinosaurs   continually   continental drift

1 Scientists have divided the history of the earth into different _____ _____.

2 The _____ Era comprised about 90% of all the earth's history.

3 The _____ Era lasted for around 300 million years.

4 The Mesozoic Era is often known as the age of the _____.

5 Scientists believe that millions of years ago, there was just one _____ on the entire earth.

6 The theory of _____ _____ explains that Earth's continents move very slowly from one position to another.

7 Much of the mantle is hot, _____ _____ which can flow like a liquid.

8 The earth's surface is _____ changing.

C Write the correct word and the meaning in Chinese.

1 ▸ a person's child or an animal's young

_____

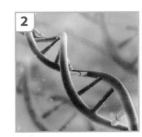
2 ▸ the basic unit of heredity

_____

3 ▸ a particular characteristic that organisms have

_____

4 ▸ a great landmass that was called Pangaea

_____

5 ▸ a large piece of the earth's surface that makes up the crust

_____

6 ▸ to develop by gradually changing or to make something do this

_____

D Match each word with the correct definition and write the meaning in Chinese.

1 heredity _____ ☐

2 trait _____ ☐

3 affect _____ ☐

4 combination _____ ☐

5 nurture _____ ☐

6 geologic _____ ☐

7 stabilize _____ ☐

8 evolve _____ ☐

9 dominate _____ ☐

10 theory _____ ☐

a. to influence
b. related to geology
c. a mixture; the state of being combined
d. care, nourishment, and encouragement given to a growing child
e. a particular characteristic that organisms have
f. the passing down of traits from parents to their offspring
g. to have power and control over someone or something
h. a set of ideas that is intended to explain something
i. to develop by gradually changing or to make something do this
j. to become stable or to make something stable

Energy
Light and Heat

Key Words

- **light wave**
- reflect
- refract
- bounce off
- reflection
- refraction
- bend
- conduction
- convection
- radiation
- conduct
- send out

Light is a form of energy that moves in waves. Light waves move 300,000 kilometers every second, so they are faster than everything in the universe. On Earth, the main source of light is the sun.

Light can be both reflected and refracted. Light travels in straight lines until it hits something. When light hits an object, the light bounces off the surface of the object. You can see your image because light bounces off the mirror and back to you. That is reflection. Refraction occurs when light goes through an object, such as water, and the light bends.

Heat is another form of energy. Heat moves through conduction, convection, and radiation. Conduction is the movement of heat by matter to carry it. Some materials, such as metals, conduct heat well. Convection is the movement of heat in a heated liquid or gas. Ovens work by convection. Finally, radiation is the movement of heat without matter to carry it. The sun sends out heat through radiation.

✔ **The Movement of Light**

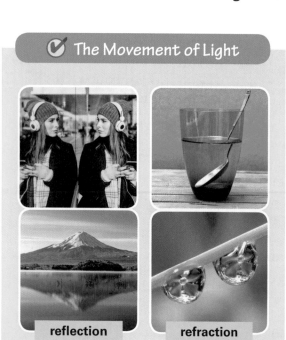

reflection

refraction

✔ **The Movement of Heat**

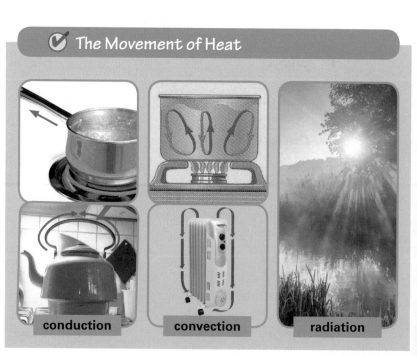

conduction

convection

radiation

Main Idea and Details

1 **What is the passage mainly about?**

　a. How light and heat are formed.　　　**b.** How light and heat move.

　c. How light and heat reflect.

2 **Many ovens transfer heat through** ＿＿＿＿＿＿.

　a. radiation　　　　　**b.** conduction　　　　　**c.** convection

3 **What happens to light when it bounces off a mirror?**

　a. It gets reflected.　　**b.** It gets conducted.　　**c.** It gets refracted.

4 **What does refracted mean?**

　a. Transferred.　　　**b.** Moved.　　　　**c.** Bended.

5 **Answer the questions.**

　a. How fast do light waves move? ＿＿＿＿＿＿＿＿＿＿＿＿＿＿＿＿＿＿＿＿＿

　b. How can heat be transferred? ＿＿＿＿＿＿＿＿＿＿＿＿＿＿＿＿＿＿＿＿＿

　c. What is conduction? ＿＿＿＿＿＿＿＿＿＿＿＿＿＿＿＿＿＿＿＿＿＿＿＿＿

6 **Complete the outline.**

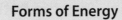

Forms of Energy

Light

- Moves in waves 300,000 kilometers every
  a ＿＿＿＿＿＿
- Reflected light bounces off a surface of an object.
- b ＿＿＿＿＿＿ light goes through an object and bends.

Heat

- Conduction = the transfer of heat by c ＿＿＿＿＿＿
- Convection = the transfer of heat in a heated liquid or gas
- Radiation = the d ＿＿＿＿＿＿ of heat without matter to carry it

Vocabulary Builder

Write the correct word and the meaning in Chinese.

▸ the bouncing back of light when it hits a surface

＿＿＿＿＿＿＿＿＿＿

▸ the bending of light when it goes through an object

＿＿＿＿＿＿＿＿＿＿

▸ the movement of heat by matter to carry it

＿＿＿＿＿＿＿＿＿＿

▸ the movement of heat in a heated liquid or gas

＿＿＿＿＿＿＿＿＿＿

Electricity is a form of energy. There are static electricity and current electricity.

Static electricity is an electric charge that builds up on an object by rubbing or friction. Static electricity is temporary and somewhat unpredictable. Current electricity is a steady stream of charges. Current electricity is more useful than static electricity because it can be more easily controlled. Current electricity runs through wires.

static electricity

Key Words

- static electricity
- current electricity
- charge
- rubbing
- friction
- temporary
- unpredictable
- steady
- circuit
- electric current
- series circuit
- parallel circuit

Let's light a bulb by using an electric circuit. A circuit is the path that an electric current follows. The electric current moves along a path that links the battery and bulb. The bulb lights only when the wire connecting it to the battery is closed. The battery provides energy to the circuit. We call this a closed circuit. An open circuit does not allow electricity to flow.

A series circuit is a circuit that has only one path for a current to follow. A parallel circuit is a circuit that has more than one path for a current to follow.

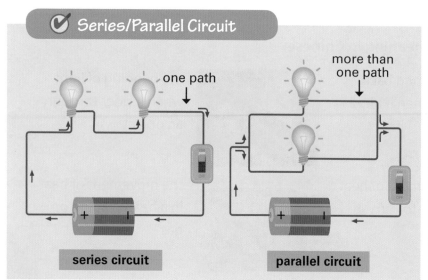

✔ **Series/Parallel Circuit**

one path

more than one path

series circuit

parallel circuit

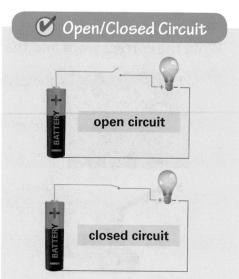

✔ **Open/Closed Circuit**

open circuit

closed circuit

Main Idea and Details

1   **What is the main idea of the passage?**

   a. Electricity can move along different types of circuits.

   b. Static electricity builds up by rubbing or friction.

   c. A parallel circuit lets electricity follow more than one path.

2   **A _____ has one path for a current to follow.**

   a. parallel circuit   **b.** closed circuit   **c.** series circuit

3   **What is current electricity?**

   a. It is electricity formed by rubbing.   **b.** It is a steady stream of charges.

   c. It is a bulb that uses an electric current.

4   **What does steady mean?**

   a. Regular.   **b.** Current.   **c.** Useful.

5   **Complete the sentences.**

   a. Current electricity is more useful than _____ electricity.

   b. An electric current follows a path called a _____.

   c. An _____ circuit does not allow electricity to flow.

6   **Complete the outline.**

```
                          Electricity
         ┌──────────────────┴──────────────────┐
  Forms of Electricity                    Types of Circuits
```

- Static electricity = temporary and somewhat ᵃ_____
- Current electricity = a ᵇ_____ stream of charges

- Series circuit = has one path for a current to follow
- ᶜ_____ circuit = has more than one path for a current to follow
- ᵈ_____ circuit = lets electricity flow
- Open circuit = does not allow electricity to flow

Vocabulary Builder

Write the correct word and the meaning in Chinese.

1 ▸ an electric charge that builds up on an object by friction

_____

2 ▸ a steady stream of charges

_____

3 ▸ a circuit that allows electricity to flow

_____

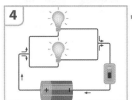

4 ▸ a circuit that has more than one path for a current to follow

_____

BATTERY +

Motion and Force

Everything in the universe moves. The sun, Earth, the planets, and even all of the stars in the universe are in constant motion.

All objects in motion have velocity. This is the rate of speed of a moving object. The position of an object is its location. Moving objects have constantly changing positions.

According to the laws of motion discovered by Sir Isaac Newton, an object in motion will continue at the same speed and in the same direction until it is acted upon by an outside force. This is known as the law of inertia.

One outside force is gravity. Gravity is the force of attraction between Earth and other objects. It pulls things toward Earth. Gravitation is the force that acts between any two objects and causes them to attract one another. Gravitation helps hold Earth in its orbit around the sun. The other planets, too, are held in their orbits by gravitation.

Friction is another force that can slow down or stop moving objects. When two bodies rub together, they create friction.

Key Words

- in motion
- velocity
- position
- laws of motion
- act upon
- law of inertia
- gravity
- gravitation
- attract
- orbit
- friction

Forces That Act Between Objects

gravity

gravitation

friction

Main Idea and Details

1 **What is the passage mainly about?**
   a. The forces that can affect objects in motion.
   b. The laws of motion discovered by Sir Isaac Newton.
   c. The effect of gravity on objects.

2 **Earth is held in its orbit around the sun by** _____.
   a. inertia   **b.** gravitation   **c.** motion

3 **What is velocity?**
   a. A force that can slow down moving objects.
   b. The rate of speed that an object moves at.
   c. The location of an object.

4 **What does attract mean?**
   a. Change.   **b.** Push.   **c.** Pull.

5 **According to the passage, which statement is true?**
   a. Velocity refers to the position of an object.
   b. Gravitation is described by the law of inertia.
   c. Two bodies rubbing together can create friction.

6 **Complete the outline.**

Motion and Force

Velocity	Inertia	Gravity and Gravitation	Friction
• Is the rate of ^{a}_____ of a moving object	• An object in ^{b}_____ continues at the same speed and in the same direction.	• Gravity = the force of ^{c}_____ between Earth and other objects • Gravitation = the force that acts between any two objects	• Is created when two objects ^{d}_____ together • Can slow down moving objects

Vocabulary Builder

Write the correct word and the meaning in Chinese.

 ► the rate of speed of a moving object

_____

 ► moving

_____

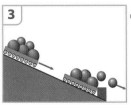 ► a law stating that a body remains at rest or in uniform motion in a straight line unless acted upon by a force

_____

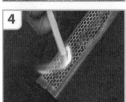 ► the force created when two objects rub together

_____

Key Words

- device
- complex
- inclined plane
- ramp
- wedge
- screw
- lever
- bar
- pliers
- pulley
- grooved rim
- crane
- wheel and axle
- doorknob
- screwdriver

We live in an age of machines. Machines are devices that do work. Many modern machines are complex. But most are based on simple machines. A simple machine has very few parts but makes it easier for people to move things. There are six types of them.

An inclined plane is a kind of ramp. It makes climbing up or down something easier.

A wedge is two inclined planes placed back to back. It can hold something in place, raise something, or split something. A doorstop is a wedge.

A screw is used to hold two objects together and to keep them from coming apart.

A lever is a simple bar that we use to move objects by applying force at another point. Scissors and pliers are levers.

A pulley is a wheel with a grooved rim that can carry a line. Pulleys, like cranes, are useful for lifting heavy objects.

A wheel and axle is a kind of lever. It has a wheel that is connected to a post called an axle. A wheel and axle changes the strength of a turning force and makes work easier. Doorknobs and screwdrivers are examples of a wheel and axle.

✓ Examples of Simple Machines

inclined plane

doorstop

wedge

screw

pulley

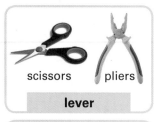

scissors   pliers

lever

doorknob   screwdriver

wheel and axle

1 What is the main idea of the passage?
a. Many machines are very complex devices.
b. Screws, levers, and pulleys are simple machines.
c. Simple machines help people do work more easily.

2 _____ **are an example of a lever.**
a. Scissors   **b.** Doorstops.   **c.** Cranes

3 What is a wedge?
a. A large wheel connected to a smaller one.
b. Two inclined planes placed back to back.
c. A simple bar that can move objects.

4 What does age mean?
a. Youth.   **b.** Factory.   **c.** Era.

5 Complete the sentences.
a. A ramp is a kind of an _____ _____.
b. A _____ can hold two objects together to keep them from moving apart.
c. A steering wheel is an example of a _____ _____ _____.

6 Complete the outline.

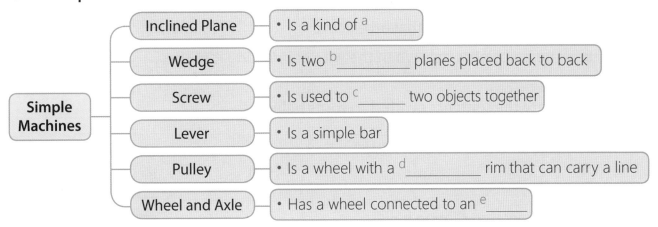

Simple Machines
- Inclined Plane — • Is a kind of ᵃ_____
- Wedge — • Is two ᵇ_____ planes placed back to back
- Screw — • Is used to ᶜ_____ two objects together
- Lever — • Is a simple bar
- Pulley — • Is a wheel with a ᵈ_____ rim that can carry a line
- Wheel and Axle — • Has a wheel connected to an ᵉ_____

Write the correct word and the meaning in Chinese.

1  ▸ a simple bar that we use to move objects by applying force at another point
_____

2 ▸ a simple machine consisting of an axle to which a wheel is fastened
_____

3 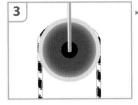 ▸ a wheel with a grooved rim that can carry a line
_____

4  ▸ two inclined planes placed back to back
_____

A

Complete the sentences with the words below.

static	convection	current	refraction
waves	reflected	rubbing	battery

1   Light is a form of energy that moves in _____.

2   Light can be both _____ and refracted.

3   _____ occurs when light goes through an object, such as water, and the light bends.

4   Heat moves through conduction, _____, and radiation.

5   Static electricity is an electric charge that builds up on an object by _____ or friction.

6   Current electricity is more useful than _____ electricity because it can be more easily controlled.

7   A circuit is the path that an electric _____ follows.

8   The bulb lights only when the wire connecting it to the _____ is closed.

B

Complete the sentences with the words below.

force	gravitation	velocity	gravity
lever	grooved	devices	inclined plane

1   All objects in motion have _____.

2   An object in motion will continue at the same speed and in the same direction until it is acted upon by an outside _____.

3   _____ is the force of attraction between Earth and other objects.

4   _____ is the force that acts between any two objects and causes them to attract one another.

5   Machines are _____ that do work.

6   An _____ _____ makes climbing up or down something easier.

7   A _____ is a simple bar that we use to move objects by applying force at another point.

8   A pulley is a wheel with a _____ rim that can carry a line.

Write the correct word and the meaning in Chinese.

 **1** ▸ the bending of light when it goes through an object

_____

 **2** ▸ the movement of heat without matter to carry it

_____

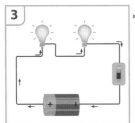 **3** ▸ a circuit that has only one path for a current to follow

_____

 **4** ▸ the force that pulls things toward Earth

_____

 **5** ▸ a wheel with a grooved rim that can carry a line

_____

 **6** ▸ two inclined planes placed back to back

_____

D

Match each word with the correct definition and write the meaning in Chinese.

1 reflection _____ ☐

2 conduct _____ ☐

3 radiation _____ ☐

4 temporary _____ ☐

5 electric circuit _____ ☐

6 velocity _____ ☐

7 gravitation _____ ☐

8 friction _____ ☐

9 device _____ ☐

10 complex _____ ☐

a. to transfer

b. lasting for a limited time

c. the rate of speed of a moving object

d. the path that an electric current follows

e. having parts that connect or go together in complicated ways

f. the force created when two objects rub together

g. the transfer of heat without matter to carry it

h. the force that acts between any two objects and pulls them together

i. the bouncing back of light when it hits a surface

j. a machine or tool that has been invented for a special job

Wrap-Up Test 2

A

Write the correct word for each sentence.

> nurturing   comprised   bounces   inherited   attraction
> charge   method   handheld   cytoplasm   recessive

1 The scientific _____ is a way that scientists use to solve a problem.

2 A magnifying glass is a small, _____ instrument that makes objects appear larger than they really are.

3 Both plant and animal cells are filled with _____.

4 _____ traits are characteristics that come from your parents.

5 The Precambrian Era _____ about 90% of all the earth's history.

6 Dominant genes are stronger than _____ genes.

7 Gravity is the force of _____ between Earth and other objects.

8 _____ and the environment can influence many traits.

9 When light hits an object, the light _____ off the surface of the object.

10 Static electricity is an electric _____ that builds up on an object by rubbing or friction.

B

Write the meanings of the words in Chinese.

1 inquiry _____
2 hypothesis _____
3 manipulate _____
4 microscopic _____
5 chloroplast _____
6 magnify _____
7 nucleus _____
8 microorganism _____
9 cell membrane _____
10 multi-celled _____
11 offspring _____
12 gene _____
13 sperm cell _____
14 supercontinent _____
15 plate _____

16 continental drift _____
17 heredity _____
18 trait _____
19 nurture _____
20 dominant _____
21 recessive _____
22 geologic _____
23 stabilize _____
24 evolve _____
25 dominate _____
26 theory _____
27 reflection _____
28 radiation _____
29 velocity _____
30 gravitation _____

3

- Mathematics
- Language
- Visual Arts
- Music

Fractions
Understanding Fractions

Key Words

- **unit fraction**
- **numerator**
- **denominator**
- **improper fraction**
- **whole number**
- **mixed number**
- **division sign**
- **equivalent fraction**
- **common factor**
- **simplest form**

A fraction is a number that names a part of a whole.

 $\frac{1}{4}$ $\frac{2}{4}$ $\frac{3}{4}$ $\frac{4}{4} = 1$

In the picture, each equal part of the whole is $\frac{1}{4}$. We call the fraction $\frac{1}{4}$ a unit fraction. A unit fraction has a numerator of 1.

When the numerator of a fraction is greater than or equal to the denominator, we call it an improper fraction. $\frac{5}{5}$, $\frac{4}{3}$, and $\frac{7}{6}$ are all improper fractions. Improper fractions can be written as either whole numbers or mixed numbers. The bar in a fraction means the same as a division sign. So, the fraction $\frac{5}{5}$ means the same thing as $5 \div 5$. $5 \div 5 = 1$. Therefore, the fraction $\frac{5}{5}$ equals the whole number 1. $\frac{4}{3} = 4 \div 3$, so $\frac{4}{3}$ can be written as the mixed number $1\frac{1}{3}$.

Some fractions, such as $\frac{1}{2}$ and $\frac{3}{6}$, name the same amount. $\frac{1}{2} = \frac{3}{6}$. Such fractions are called equivalent fractions. You can make an equivalent fraction by multiplying or dividing the numerator and denominator by the same number.

$$\frac{1}{2} = \frac{1 \times 3}{2 \times 3} = \frac{3}{6} \qquad \frac{3}{6} = \frac{3 \div 3}{6 \div 3} = \frac{1}{2} \qquad$$  $\frac{1}{2} = \frac{3}{6}$

A fraction is in its simplest form when its numerator and denominator have no common factor greater than 1. A common factor is a number that the numerator and denominator can both be divided by. For example, $\frac{4}{8} = \frac{4 \div 4}{8 \div 4} = \frac{1}{2}$. So, 4 is a common factor of 4 and 8. The simplest form of $\frac{4}{8}$ is $\frac{1}{2}$.

The simplest form?

The largest number that can divide both the numerator and the denominator is called the greatest common factor. For example, $\frac{12}{16}$ can be divided by both 2 and 4.

$$\frac{12}{16} = \frac{12 \div 2}{16 \div 2} = \frac{6}{8} \quad \text{or} \quad \frac{12}{16} = \frac{12 \div 4}{16 \div 4} = \frac{3}{4}$$

2 and 4 are common factors, and 4 is the greatest common factor of 12 and 16.

Main Idea and Details

1 **What is the main idea of the passage?**

a. Fractions have both a numerator and a denominator.

b. Two fractions usually have a common denominator.

c. There are many different types of fractions.

2 **The greatest common factor of $\frac{12}{16}$ is _____.**

a. 2   **b.** 3   **c.** 4

3 **Which of the following is a mixed number?**

a. 2   **b.** $2\frac{1}{3}$ **c.** $\frac{2}{2}$

4 **What does names mean?**

a. Selects.   **b.** Represents.   **c.** Lists.

5 **Complete the sentences.**

a. $\frac{4}{4}$, $\frac{6}{2}$, and $\frac{8}{7}$ are all _____ fractions.

b. In a fraction, the _____ has the same meaning as a division sign.

c. $\frac{2}{4}$ and $\frac{4}{8}$ are _____ fractions.

6 **Complete the outline.**

Fractions

Improper Fractions

Equivalent Fractions

Common Factors

- Are when the numerator is ᵃ_____ than or equal to the denominator
- $\frac{5}{5}$, $\frac{4}{3}$, and $\frac{7}{6}$ are improper fractions.

- Are fractions that name the same ᵇ_____
- $\frac{1}{2}$ and $\frac{3}{6}$ are equivalent fractions.

- Are numbers that the numerator and ᶜ_____ can both be divided by
- 2 and ᵈ____ are common factors of $\frac{4}{8}$.

Vocabulary Builder

Write the correct word and the meaning in Chinese.

1 $\frac{5}{2}$, $\frac{9}{8}$ ▸ a fraction that has a value greater than 1

_____

2 $\frac{1}{3}$, $\frac{1}{6}$ ▸ a fraction that has a numerator of 1

_____

3 $1\frac{3}{4}$ ▸ a number consisting of a whole number and a proper fraction

_____

4 $\frac{9}{12} \rightarrow \frac{3}{4}$ ▸ a fraction in its lowest term

_____

Word Problems With Fractions

Key Words

- greatest common factor
- solution
- reduce
- common denominator
- unlike fractions

Ah-ha!

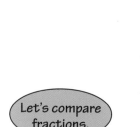

Let's compare fractions.

❶ What are the common factors and the greatest common factor of $\frac{16}{20}$?

Solution $\frac{16 \div 2}{20 \div 2} = \frac{8}{10}$. $\frac{16 \div 4}{20 \div 4} = \frac{4}{5}$.

Since $\frac{16}{20}$ can be divided by both 2 and 4, 2 and 4 are common factors of 16 and 20. And 4 is the greatest common factor of $\frac{16}{20}$.

❷ Reduce the fraction $\frac{12}{18}$ to its simplest form.

Solution 1 Divide the numerator and denominator by 2.

$\frac{12}{18} = \frac{12 \div 2}{18 \div 2} = \frac{6}{9}$.

Since $\frac{6}{9}$ is not in its simplest form, you can go further. Divide the numerator and denominator by 3. $\frac{6 \div 3}{9 \div 3} = \frac{2}{3}$.

There are no more common factors greater than 1. So, the simplest form of $\frac{12}{18} = \frac{2}{3}$.

Solution 2 Divide the numerator and denominator by the greatest common factor. Then you can find the simplest form in one step. $\frac{12 \div 6}{18 \div 6} = \frac{2}{3}$. So, the simplest form of $\frac{12}{18} = \frac{2}{3}$.

❸ Compare the fractions $\frac{2}{5}$ and $\frac{4}{5}$.

Solution $\frac{2}{5} < \frac{4}{5}$. $\frac{4}{5}$ is greater than $\frac{2}{5}$.

When you compare fractions with common denominators, you only compare the numerators.

❹ Compare the fractions $\frac{2}{3}$ and $\frac{3}{6}$.

Solution $\frac{2}{3} = \frac{2 \times 2}{3 \times 2} = \frac{4}{6}$. $\frac{4}{6} > \frac{3}{6}$.

So, $\frac{2}{3}$ is greater than $\frac{3}{6}$. To compare unlike fractions, you need to make their denominators the same. Therefore, find the equivalent fraction for $\frac{2}{3}$ with a denominator of 6 first. Once their denominators are the same, you can easily compare them.

Main Idea and Details

1 **What is the passage mainly about?**

    a. How to solve problems with fractions.

    b. How to compare two fractions.

    c. How to divide one fraction into another.

2 **The simplest form of $\frac{12}{18}$ is _____.**

    a. $\frac{1}{3}$ **b.** $\frac{2}{3}$ **c.** $\frac{3}{3}$

3 **Which is greater, $\frac{2}{5}$ or $\frac{4}{5}$?**

    a. $\frac{2}{5}$ **b.** $\frac{4}{5}$ **c.** They have the same value.

4 **What does further mean?**

    a. More.   **b.** Less.   **c.** Many.

5 **According to the passage, which statement is true?**

    a. The greatest common factor of $\frac{16}{20}$ is 2.

    b. The simplest form of $\frac{12}{18}$ is $\frac{3}{4}$.

    c. $\frac{2}{3}$ is greater than $\frac{3}{6}$.

6 **Complete the sentences.**

    a. To compare fractions with common denominators, compare only the

    _____.

    b. To find the simplest form, divide the numerator and denominator by the

    _____ _____ _____.

    c. To compare unlike fractions, make their _____ the same.

Vocabulary Builder

Write the correct word and the meaning in Chinese.

1
$$\frac{1}{3} + \frac{1}{4}$$
$$= \frac{4}{12} + \frac{3}{12}$$
$$= \frac{7}{12}$$

▸ the process of finding an answer to a problem or puzzle

_____

2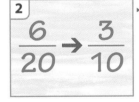

▸ to convert (a fraction) to its simplest form

_____

3
$$\frac{2}{5}, \frac{3}{5}, \frac{4}{5}$$

▸ the same denominator

_____

4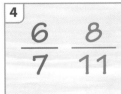

▸ fractions with different denominators

_____

Lines and Angles

Key Words

- line segment
- ray
- vertex
- measuring tool
- protractor
- right angle
- perpendicular lines
- intersect
- acute angle
- obtuse angle
- straight angle

When two lines, line segments, or rays meet at a common point, they form an angle. The point where they come together is called a vertex. Here is angle ABC.

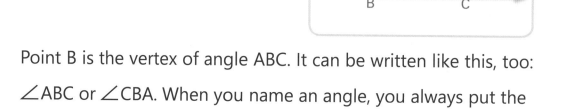

Point B is the vertex of angle ABC. It can be written like this, too: ∠ABC or ∠CBA. When you name an angle, you always put the vertex in the middle.

The size of an angle is measured in degrees(°). When we measure angles, we use a measuring tool called a protractor. An angle can measure anywhere from 0 to 180 degrees.

There are four types of angles. A right angle measures exactly 90°. A right angle forms when perpendicular lines intersect. An acute angle is less than a right angle. It measures greater than 0° and less than 90°. An obtuse angle is greater than a right angle. It measures greater than 90° and less than 180°. A straight angle measures 180°. A straight angle forms a line.

Types of Angles

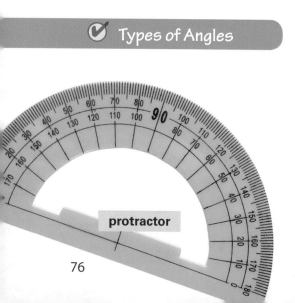

protractor

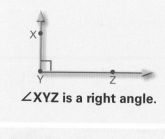

∠XYZ is a right angle.

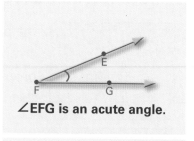

∠EFG is an acute angle.

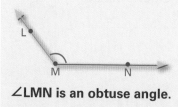

∠LMN is an obtuse angle.

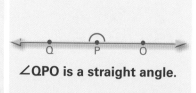

∠QPO is a straight angle.

1 **What is the passage mainly about?**

a. How to make measurements with a protractor.

b. The angles that are formed by lines.

c. The difference between acute and obtuse angles.

2 **A right angle measures** _____.

a. 0°　　　　　　　　b. 90°　　　　　　　　c. 180°

3 **What is a vertex?**

a. A right angle.

b. A measurement gained from a protractor.

c. A point where two lines come together.

4 **What does segments mean?**

a. Angles.　　　　b. Measurements.　　　　c. Pieces.

5 **Answer the questions.**

a. What can measure an angle? _____

b. What is an acute angle? _____

c. What is an obtuse angle? _____

6 **Complete the outline.**

Angles

Forming an Angle	Measuring an Angle	Types of Angles
• Form when two lines, line segments, or rays meet at a common point • The common point is called a a _____.	• Are measured in b_____ • Use a protractor • Can measure from 0° to 180°	• Right angle = exactly 90° • c _____ _____ = greater than 0° and less than 90° • Obtuse angle = greater than 90° and less than 180° • Straight angle = exactly d_____

Write the correct word and the meaning in Chinese.

1 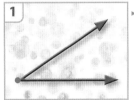 ▸ the point where two lines join at an angle

_____

2  ▸ a tool used to measure angles

_____

3 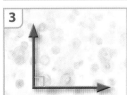 ▸ lines that intersect at a right angle

_____

4 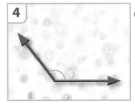 ▸ an angle that is greater than 90° and less than 180°

_____

Polygons, Triangles, and Circles

Key Words

- **polygon**
- **parallelogram**
- **rhombus**
- **trapezoid**
- **equilateral triangle**
- **isosceles triangle**
- **scalene triangle**
- **chord**
- **diameter**
- **bisect**
- **radius**

A polygon is a closed figure with three or more sides. A polygon with four sides can be a square, rectangle, parallelogram, rhombus, or trapezoid. A polygon with five sides is a pentagon, and one with six sides is a hexagon.

A polygon with three sides is a triangle. There are several types of triangles. A triangle with three equal sides is an equilateral triangle. A triangle with two equal sides is an isosceles triangle. And a triangle with three sides that are all unequal is a scalene triangle.

Also, all the angles in an acute triangle are acute. A right triangle has one right angle. And an obtuse triangle has one obtuse angle.

A circle is a closed rounded figure in which every point is the same distance from the center. Circles have different parts. A chord is a line segment that connects two points on the circle. The diameter is a chord that bisects a circle. And the radius is a line segment with one endpoint at the center of a circle and the other endpoint on the circle. It is half the length of the diameter.

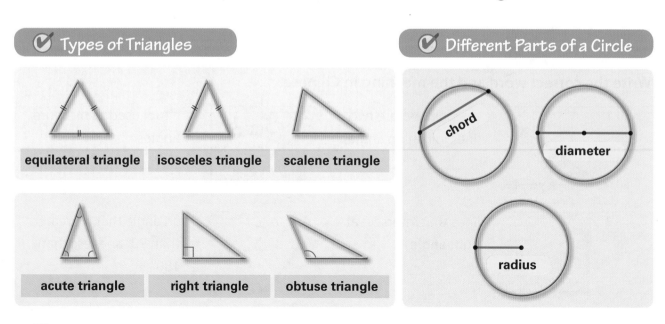

✔ Types of Triangles	✔ Different Parts of a Circle
equilateral triangle isosceles triangle scalene triangle	chord diameter
acute triangle right triangle obtuse triangle	radius

1 **What is the main idea of the passage?**
    a. There are many kinds of polygons and circles.
    b. There are several kinds of triangles.
    c. A circle is made from a single line.

2 **A rhombus has _____ sides.**
    a. three   **b.** four   **c.** five

3 **What is a scalene triangle?**
    a. A triangle with no equal sides.   **b.** A triangle with two equal sides.
    c. A triangle with three equal sides.

4 **What does bisects mean?**
    a. Expands.   **b.** Cuts.   **c.** Halves.

5 **Complete the sentences.**
    a. A parallelogram is a _____ with four sides.
    b. An _____ triangle has three equal sides.
    c. The _____ is half the length of the diameter.

6 **Complete the outline.**

Polygons

Four-Sided Polygons	Triangles	Circles
• Squares, rectangles, parallelograms, ᵃ_____, and trapezoids	• Have three sides • Equilateral triangle, isosceles triangle, and ᵇ_____ triangle • Acute triangle, ᶜ_____ triangle, and right triangle	• Is a closed round figure • ᵈ_____ = a line segment connecting two points on the circle • Diameter = a chord that bisects the circle • Radius = half the length of the diameter

Write the correct word and the meaning in Chinese.

1 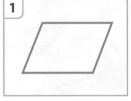 ▸ a four-sided figure in which the opposite sides are parallel

_____

2 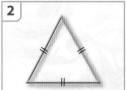 ▸ a triangle with three equal sides

_____

3 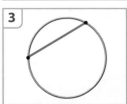 ▸ a line segment that connects two points on the circle

_____

4 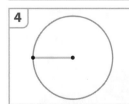 ▸ a straight line from the center of a circle to any point on the outer edge

_____

Vocabulary **Review 7**

A

Complete the sentences with the words below.

> equivalent   numerator   unlike   division sign
> divided   denominators   simplest   common factors

1   When the _____ of a fraction is greater than or equal to the denominator, we call it an improper fraction.

2   The bar in a fraction means the same as a _____ _____.

3   You can make an _____ fraction by multiplying or dividing the numerator and denominator by the same number.

4   A common factor is a number that the numerator and denominator can both be _____ by.

5   Since $\frac{16}{20}$ can be divided by both 2 and 4, 2 and 4 are _____ _____ of 16 and 20.

6   Reduce the fraction $\frac{12}{18}$ to its _____ form.

7   When you compare fractions with common _____, you only compare the numerators.

8   To compare _____ fractions, you need to make their denominators the same.

B

Complete the sentences with the words below.

> bisects   chord   equilateral   acute angle
> polygon   angle   perpendicular   right angle

1   When two lines, line segments, or rays meet at a common point, they form an _____.

2   A right angle forms when _____ lines intersect.

3   An _____ _____ measures greater than 0° and less than 90°.

4   An obtuse angle is greater than a _____ _____.

5   A _____ is a closed figure with three or more sides.

6   A triangle with three equal sides is an _____ triangle.

7   A _____ is a line segment that connects two points on the circle.

8   The diameter is a chord that _____ a circle.

Write the correct word and the meaning in Chinese.

1

$$\frac{5}{2} \quad \frac{9}{8}$$

▸ a fraction that has a value greater than 1

_____

2

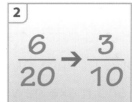

▸ to convert (a fraction) to its simplest form

_____

3

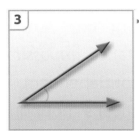

▸ an angle that is less than a right angle

_____

4

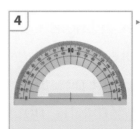

▸ a tool used to measure angles

_____

5

▸ a four-sided figure in which the opposite sides are parallel

_____

6

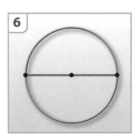

▸ a chord that bisects a circle

_____

D

Match each word with the correct definition and write the meaning in Chinese.

1   common factor   _____ ☐

2   simplest form   _____ ☐

3   solution   _____ ☐

4   reduce   _____ ☐

5   common denominator   _____ ☐

6   unlike fractions   _____ ☐

7   right angle   _____ ☐

8   obtuse angle   _____ ☐

9   isosceles triangle   _____ ☐

10   diameter   _____ ☐

a. an angle that is 90°

b. the same denominator

c. a fraction in its lowest term

d. a triangle with two equal sides

e. fractions with different denominators

f. the process of finding an answer to a problem or puzzle

g. to decrease; to convert (a fraction) to its simplest form

h. a cord that passes through the center of a circle

i. an angle that is greater than 90° and less than 180°

j. a number that the numerator and denominator can both be divided by

Prefixes and Suffixes

29

Prefixes and suffixes are groups of letters that are added to the fronts or ends of words. They often add extra meanings to words and make new words.

Key Words

- prefix
- suffix
- extra
- common
- beforehand
- continuous form
- figure out
- break down
- root

A prefix goes at the beginning of a word. There are many prefixes in English. Some prefixes mean "no" or "not." Among them are *im-*, *in-*, *un-*, *dis-*, and *non-*. For instance, *impossible* means "not possible," *independent* means "not dependent," *unhappy* means "not happy," and *dishonest* means "not honest." Here are some other common prefixes and their meanings:

pre-	= before	**pre**view
fore-	= before, beforehand	**fore**cast, **fore**ground
mid-	= middle	**mid**term
inter-	= between, among	**inter**mediate, **inter**national
re-	= again	**re**peat, **re**do
mis-	= wrong, wrongly	**mis**spell, **mis**take

A suffix goes at the end of a word. There are many suffixes in English. Two very common suffixes are *-ed* and *-ing*. *-ed* makes the past tense form of a verb. And *-ing* makes the continuous form of a verb. Here are some other common suffixes and their meanings:

-er	= a person who	teach**er**, farm**er**
-en	= made of	gold**en**
-ful	= full of	wonder**ful**
-able	= able to be done	wash**able**
-less	= without	care**less**, pain**less**

It is useful to know commonly used prefixes and suffixes. Sometimes you can figure out the meanings of some difficult words by breaking them down into prefixes, roots, and suffixes.

1 **What is the main idea of the passage?**

　　a. People often use both prefixes and suffixes.

　　b. Prefixes and suffixes can make new words.

　　c. Prefixes and suffixes are useful to understanding some words.

2 **The prefix** ＿＿＿＿＿＿＿ **means "between."**

　　a. inter-　　　　　　**b.** fore-　　　　　　**c.** mid-

3 **What does -*en* mean?**

　　a. Able to be done.　　**b.** Without.　　　　**c.** Made of.

4 **What does extra mean?**

　　a. Bonus.　　　　　　**b.** Unique.　　　　　**c.** Additional.

5 **According to the passage, which statement is true?**

　　a. The prefixes *in-*, *un-*, and *non-* all mean "not."

　　b. The prefix *fore-* means "again."

　　c. The suffix *-ed* makes the continuous form of a verb.

6 **Complete the outline.**

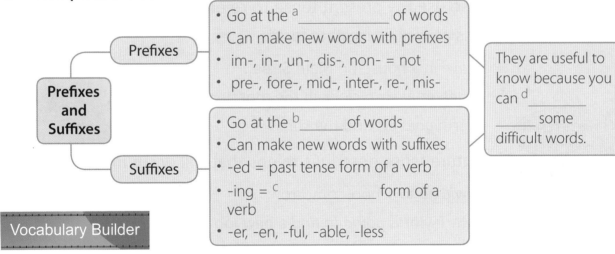

- Go at the ª＿＿＿＿＿ of words
- Can make new words with prefixes
- im-, in-, un-, dis-, non- = not
- pre-, fore-, mid-, inter-, re-, mis-

They are useful to know because you can ᵈ＿＿＿＿ ＿＿＿＿ some difficult words.

- Go at the ᵇ＿＿＿ of words
- Can make new words with suffixes
- -ed = past tense form of a verb
- -ing = ᶜ＿＿＿＿＿ form of a verb
- -er, -en, -ful, -able, -less

Write the correct word and the meaning in Chinese.

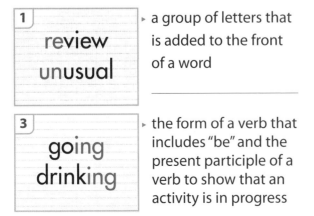

1

review
unusual

▸ a group of letters that is added to the front of a word

_____

2

beautiful
worker

▸ a group of letters that is added to the end of a word

_____

3

going
drinking

▸ the form of a verb that includes "be" and the present participle of a verb to show that an activity is in progress

_____

4

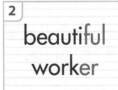

midnight
endless

▸ the basic part of a word that shows its main meaning

_____

Key Words

- tense
- take place
- past tense
- present tense
- future tense
- describe
- refer to
- repeated
- habitual
- state
- continuous tense
- perfect tense

In English, all sentences have a verb. A verb shows the action in the sentence. Verbs can tell about actions that are happening now, actions that happened before, and actions that will happen later. We call this a tense. The tense shows the time in which an action takes place. There are three main verb tenses: the past tense, the present tense, and the future tense.

The past tense describes things that have already happened.

> I *met* my friend yesterday.
> She *lived* in New York City ten years ago.

We met yesterday.

The present tense describes things that are happening now. We also use the present tense to refer to repeated or habitual actions as well as to state facts.

> I *live* in a house on Main Street.
> I *get* up at six o'clock in the morning.
> Earth *goes* around the sun.

I get up early.

I'll go to school tomorrow.

The future tense describes things that will occur in the future.

> I *will go* to school tomorrow.
> Mr. Taylor *is going to find* a new job next week.

Those are the three basic tenses. There are also different forms of each tense: the continuous tense and perfect tense. We can use the past, present, and future continuous tenses. We can also use the past, present, and future perfect tenses.

There are 12 main tenses in English.

Basic Tense	Continuous Tense	Perfect Tense
past	past continuous	past perfect
present	present continuous	present perfect
future	future continuous	future perfect

Main Idea and Details

1 **What is the main idea of the passage?**

a. Some people use the continuous and perfect tenses.

b. The present and future tenses are different from each other.

c. There are many different verb tenses in English.

2 **We describe repeated or habitual actions with the _____.**

a. past tense   **b.** present tense   **c.** continuous tense

3 **Which tense describes actions that have already happened?**

a. The future tense.   **b.** The perfect tense.   **c.** The past tense.

4 **What does habitual mean?**

a. Extreme.   **b.** Usual.   **c.** Past.

5 **Answer the questions.**

a. What does a verb do? _____

b. What are the three main tenses? _____

c. What does the future tense describe? _____

6 **Complete the outline.**

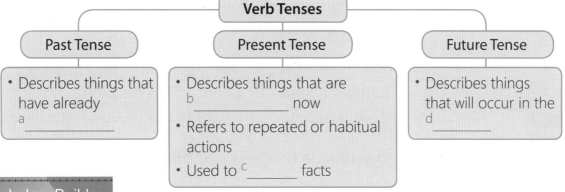

Verb Tenses

Past Tense
- Describes things that have already
  a _____

Present Tense
- Describes things that are
  b _____ now
- Refers to repeated or habitual actions
- Used to c _____ facts

Future Tense
- Describes things that will occur in the
  d _____

Vocabulary Builder

Write the correct word and the meaning in Chinese.

1 He is going to find a new job next week.

▸ a tense used to describe things that will occur in the future

_____

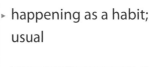

2 Earth goes around the sun.

▸ a tense used to describe things that are happening now and to state facts

_____

3 The sun rises in the east.

▸ done or happening again and again

_____

4

▸ happening as a habit; usual

_____

Grammar
Complete Sentences

A sentence is a group of words that expresses a complete thought. A complete sentence has a subject and a predicate. The subject tells what the sentence is about. The predicate tells what the subject of the sentence is or does.

Key Words

- subject
- predicate
- part of speech
- sentence fragment
- incomplete sentence
- compound sentence
- comma
- conjunction
- run-on sentence

Subject	Predicate
John	eats.
She	watches TV.
My big brother	goes to school every day.

The subject is usually a noun or a pronoun, and it usually comes at the beginning of the sentence. The predicate must include a verb and may include other parts of speech.

A sentence fragment is a part of a sentence or an incomplete sentence. It is missing either a subject or a verb, and it does not express a complete thought.

Sentence Fragment	Complete Sentence
Went to the movies	I went to the movies.
Movies last weekend	I went to the movies last weekend.

A compound sentence contains two or more complete sentences. The sentences are joined by a comma and a conjunction like *and*, *but*, *so*, and *or*.

> I like oranges, **and** my sister likes oranges, too.
> We stayed home, **but** James went out.

If you do not use a comma or a conjunction when you combine two sentences, you make a run-on sentence.

Run-on Sentence	Complete Sentence
Be careful don't move.	Be careful, and don't move.
I speak English John speaks Chinese.	I speak English, and John speaks Chinese.
	I speak English. John speaks Chinese.

Main Idea and Details

1 **What is the passage mainly about?**

   a. Why to avoid run-on sentences.   **b.** How to write complete sentences.

   c. What compound sentences are.

2 *And*, *but*, and *so* are examples of _____.

   a. conjunctions   **b.** commas   **c.** compound sentences

3 **What is a run-on sentence?**

   a. Two sentences that are connected with a conjunction.

   b. Two sentences that both have a subject and a predicate.

   c. Two combined sentences that do not have a comma or conjunction.

4 **What does fragment mean?**

   a. Example.   **b.** Compound.   **c.** Section.

5 **Complete the sentences.**

   a. A complete sentence must have both a _____ and a predicate.

   b. A part of a sentence is called a sentence _____.

   c. Two or more sentences combined into one form a _____ sentence.

6 **Complete the outline.**

```
                          ┌─────────────┐
                          │  Sentences  │
                          └─────────────┘
```

What They Are	Sentence Fragments	Compound Sentences	Run-on Sentences
• Groups of words that express complete thoughts • Have a ᵃ_____ and a predicate	• Parts of sentences or ᵇ_____ sentences • Are missing a subject or a verb	• Two or more complete sentences joined together • Are joined by a ᶜ_____ and a conjunction	• Two combined sentences that do not have a comma or a ᵈ_____

Vocabulary Builder

Write the correct word and the meaning in Chinese.

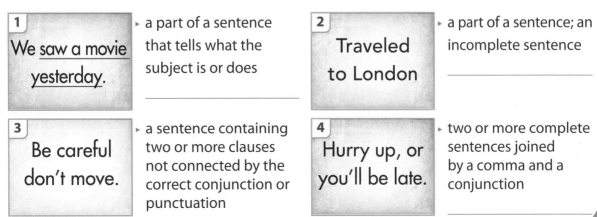

1 We saw a movie yesterday. ▸ a part of a sentence that tells what the subject is or does
_____

2 Traveled to London ▸ a part of a sentence; an incomplete sentence
_____

3 Be careful don't move. ▸ a sentence containing two or more clauses not connected by the correct conjunction or punctuation
_____

4 Hurry up, or you'll be late. ▸ two or more complete sentences joined by a comma and a conjunction
_____

Read the paragraph below. There are 9 mistakes in the paragraph. Use proofreading marks to correct the mistakes.

Key Words

- paragraph
- proofread
- mark
- incorrect
- insert
- punctuation
- delete
- capitalize
- lowercase
- amusement park
- roller coaster
- ride
- bumper car
- get crowded

Proofreading Marks

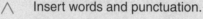

~~go~~ *went*   Draw a line through each incorrect word and write the correct word above it.

∧   Insert words and punctuation.

   Delete incorrect words and punctuation.

≡   Capitalize a letter.

/   Lowercase a letter.

Jessica always does something exciting every weekend. Last saturday, she decided to visit the amusement park with her friend Tina. Jessica and Tina took the bus to the amusement park. They got there early in the morning because there were few people there until noon. This way, did not have to wait in line very long.

Jessica loves Roller coasters so does Tina. They rode on a couple of them, and then they rode on the bumper cars, too. They started to get tired so they bought some snacks and drinks and sat down for a while. Jessica wanted to go on some more rides but Tina didn't. The park was beginning to get crowded, so they had to wait longer to go on each each ride. Jessica and Tina decided to go home. They had a fun day. They go to the bus stop and then rode back to their homes.

roller coaster

bumper car

Main Idea and Details

1 **What is the passage mainly about?**

  a. Making corrections to incorrect words and sentences.

  b. Describing a recent trip to the amusement park.

  c. Showing how to write a diary entry.

2 **You can draw a line through a word to show that it is** _____

  a. too long   **b.** incorrect   **c.** correct

3 **What do you use ∧ for?**

  a. To insert words and punctuation.

  b. To delete incorrect words.

  c. To start a new sentence.

4 **What does crowded mean?**

  a. Boring.   **b.** Expensive.   **c.** Full.

5 **According to the passage, which statement is true?**

  a. Jessica and Tina went to the amusement park on Sunday.

  b. Both Jessica and Tina like roller coasters.

  c. Tina wanted to go on many rides at the amusement park.

6 **Complete the sentences.**

  a. The proofreading mark ≡ means you should _____ the letter.

  b. The proofreading mark ℘ means you should _____ incorrect words and punctuation.

  c. The proofreading mark / means you should _____ the letter.

Vocabulary Builder

Write the correct word and the meaning in Chinese.

1 visits
He ~~visit~~ us every Sunday.

▸ to read and correct mistakes in (a written or printed piece of writing)

_____

2 I live in
s͟eattle.

▸ to write something using capital letters

_____

3 I smiled, he frowned.∧but

▸ to put something inside

_____

4 ! ? .
, ;

▸ the marks (such as commas) in a piece of writing that make its meaning clear

_____

A

Complete the sentences with the words below.

repeated	action	added	prefixes
takes place	future	describes	breaking

1   Prefixes and suffixes are groups of letters that are _____ to the fronts or ends of words.

2   It is useful to know commonly used _____ and suffixes.

3   Sometimes you can figure out the meanings of some difficult words by _____ them down into prefixes, roots, and suffixes.

4   A verb shows the _____ in the sentence.

5   The tense shows the time in which an action _____ _____.

6   The past tense _____ things that have already happened.

7   We use the present tense to refer to _____ or habitual actions as well as to state facts.

8   The future tense describes things that will occur in the _____.

B

Complete the sentences with the words below.

predicate	compound	complete	incorrect
conjunction	fragment	proofreading	verb

1   A sentence is a group of words that expresses a _____ thought.

2   A complete sentence has a subject and a _____.

3   The predicate must include a _____ and may include other parts of speech.

4   A sentence _____ is a part of a sentence or an incomplete sentence.

5   A _____ sentence contains two or more complete sentences.

6   If you do not use a comma or a _____ when you combine two sentences, you make a run-on sentence.

7   Use _____ marks to correct the mistakes in the paragraph.

8   Draw a line through each _____ word and write the correct word above it.

C Write the correct word and the meaning in Chinese.

1

beautiful
worker

▸ a group of letters that is added to the end of a word

_____

2

midnight
endless

▸ the basic part of a word that shows its main meaning

_____

3

Traveled
to London

▸ a part of a sentence; an incomplete sentence

_____

4

and or
     so
but

▸ a word such as "and" or "but" that connects two sentences or phrases

_____

5

visits
He ~~visit~~ us
every Sunday.

▸ reading and making corrections on a proof or other copy of a text

_____

6

▸ happening as a habit; usual

_____

D Match each word with the correct definition and write the meaning in Chinese.

1 prefix _____ ☐

2 break down _____ ☐

3 root _____ ☐

4 take place _____ ☐

5 describe _____ ☐

6 habitual _____ ☐

7 predicate _____ ☐

8 compound sentence _____ ☐

9 incorrect _____ ☐

10 insert _____ ☐

a. to divide into parts

b. to occur; to happen

c. not correct; wrong

d. to put something inside

e. happening as a habit; usual

f. the basic part of a word that shows its main meaning

g. a part of a sentence that tells what the subject is or does

h. a group of letters that is added to the front of a word

i. to say what someone or something is like by giving details

j. two or more complete sentences joined by a comma and a conjunction

Key Words

- **Gothic**
- **cathedral**
- **spire**
- **grandeur**
- **inspire**
- **depict**
- **awe-inspiring**
- **buttress**
- **brace**
- **demon**
- **gargoyle**
- **medieval**
- **illuminated manuscript**
- **monk**

The Middle Ages lasted for around 1,000 years until 1400s. During this time, many magnificent Gothic cathedrals were built in Europe, and most art was influenced by the Church.

Many Gothic cathedrals had towers and spires that reached high in the air. The height and grandeur of cathedrals inspired people to be more religious. Tall ceilings, paintings, and stained-glass windows depicting stories from the Bible also created awe-inspiring spaces.

Another feature of Gothic cathedrals was their buttresses. Because the cathedrals were so tall and enormous, stone braces called buttresses supported the cathedrals and kept them from collapsing. Stone statues of demons called gargoyles were often found on cathedrals, too. Notre Dame Cathedral and Chartres Cathedral in France are two famous medieval cathedrals.

Some of the most beautiful medieval art is also found in books called illuminated manuscripts. During the Middle Ages, books were copied by hand by monks. Monks illuminated many of the pages by drawing pictures with bits of real gold and silver in the books. The *Book of Kells* is one famous illuminated manuscript.

✅ Some Features of Gothic Cathedrals

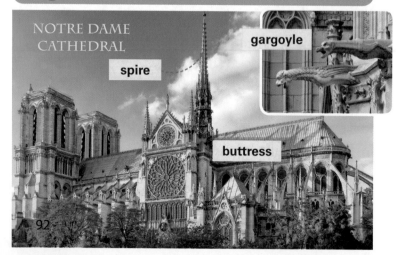

NOTRE DAME CATHEDRAL

gargoyle

spire

buttress

✅ Illuminated Manuscripts

from the *Book of Kells*

Main Idea and Details

1 **What is the passage mainly about?**

    a. Different kinds of medieval art.   **b.** How monks made illuminated manuscripts.

    c. Gothic cathedrals and their artworks.

2 **Gargoyles are stone _____ of demons often found on cathedrals.**

    a. books   **b.** paintings   **c.** statues

3 **What is the *Book of Kells*?**

    a. An illuminated manuscript.   **b.** A place where many monks live.

    c. A famous Gothic cathedral.

4 **What does grandeur mean?**

    a. Sharpness.   **b.** Majesty.   **c.** Appearance.

5 **Answer the questions.**

    a. What supported Gothic cathedrals? _____

    b. What created awe-inspiring spaces in Gothic cathedrals?

    _____

    c. How did people make books in the Middle Ages? _____

6 **Complete the outline.**

Medieval Art

Gothic Cathedrals

- Had high towers and spires
- Had tall ᵃ_____, paintings, and stained-glass windows
- Had buttresses to support them
- Had stone ᵇ_____ of gargoyles
- Notre Dame ᶜ_____ and Chartres Cathedral

Illuminated Manuscripts

- Contain beautiful artwork
- Books were copied ᵈ____ _____.
- Monks drew pictures with bits of real gold and silver.
- The *Book of Kells* = famous ᵉ_____ manuscript

Vocabulary Builder

Write the correct word and the meaning in Chinese.

 **1** ▸ a stone statue of an ugly creature, used mainly on old churches for directing water away from the roof

_____

 **2** ▸ making one feel awe

_____

 **3** ▸ a stone brace that supports a cathedral so that it does not collapse

_____

 **4** ▸ a very old book or document written by hand before books began to be printed

_____

Key Words

- architecture
- minaret
- mosque
- worship
- dome
- rounded
- mask
- ancestor
- carve
- terra cotta
- brass
- depict

Art from around the world has various styles and looks.

During the Middle Ages, Muslims from North Africa conquered much of Spain. They developed a very different architecture style from the Gothic style.

One of the main features of Islamic architecture is the minaret. Most mosques—Islamic houses of worship—have four minarets. These are tall towers found at each of the four corners of a mosque. Many Islamic buildings have domes, too. A dome is a rounded roof or a ceiling on a building. The Dome of the Rock in Jerusalem, Israel, and the Taj Mahal in Agra, India, are two beautiful examples of Islamic architecture.

In Africa, artists made both statues and masks. A long time ago, many African people did not write down their histories. They remembered things from the past by singing songs, dancing, and making works of art. To remember their ancestors, they carved sculptures and made many masks. The sculptures were typically made of terra cotta or brass. They depicted people and animals. The masks showed various faces. African people wore them when they performed mask dances.

✓ **Islamic Architecture**

✓ **Statues and Masks From Africa**

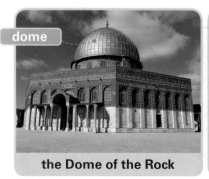

dome

the Dome of the Rock

minaret

the Taj Mahal

masks

sculptures

Main Idea and Details

1 **What is the main idea of the passage?**

a. The art of Islam was more interesting than that of Africa.

b. Islam and Africa had their own unique styles of art.

c. African people used their masks in various mask dances.

2 **Most African sculptures were made of _____ or brass.**

a. gold   **b.** silver   **c.** terra cotta

3 **What do most mosques have?**

a. 4 minarets.   **b.** 4 domes.   **c.** 4 ceilings.

4 **What does carved mean?**

a. Cut.   **b.** Sliced.   **c.** Sewed.

5 **Complete the sentences.**

a. A minaret is a tall tower often found at each corner of a _____.

b. _____ are a feature on the roofs of many Islamic buildings.

c. Africans made many masks to honor their _____.

6 **Complete the outline.**

Art from around the World

Islamic Art

• Minaret = a tall ᵃ_____ at each corner of a mosque
• Dome = a rounded ᵇ_____ or ceiling on a building
• The Dome of the Rock and the Taj Mahal = beautiful Islamic architecture

African Art

• Made sculptures and ᶜ_____
• Remembered history by singing songs, dancing, and making works of art
• Carved ᵈ_____ of terra cotta and brass
• Made masks showing various faces

Vocabulary Builder

Write the correct word and the meaning in Chinese.

1 ▸ a Muslim place of worship

_____

2 ▸ a tall tower found at each of the four corners of a mosque

_____

3 ▸ a yellow metal that is made by combining copper and zinc

_____

4 ▸ red clay baked in a hot fire

_____

People around the world, no matter what language they speak, can read music and sing or play it. This is all thanks to musical notation.

Songwriters and composers use a special kind of writing called "notation" to write down their music. Once you can read the notation, you can freely sing and play music no matter how complicated it is.

Let's look at some parts of musical notation. Musical notes are written on a staff. The notes basically tell us the rhythm, length, and pitch of the music. Sometimes, a musical note may have a dot over it. We call it a dotted note. It tells the musician to increase the length of the note by one half. Sometimes, there is a curved line connecting two notes. This line is called a tie. It tells the musician to continue to hold the first note through the time of the second.

At the beginning of each piece of music is the time signature. It is always two numbers, such as $\frac{4}{4}$, $\frac{3}{4}$, or $\frac{2}{4}$. The time signature shows the meter or beat of the piece and indicates how the musician should play it.

Composers often divide their music into measures. To show where a measure begins and ends, they use a single bar line. To show where a piece of music is finished, they use a double bar line.

Key Words

- musical notation
- rhythm
- dotted note
- tie
- time signature
- meter
- beat
- piece
- measure
- single bar line
- double bar line

✓ Musical Notation

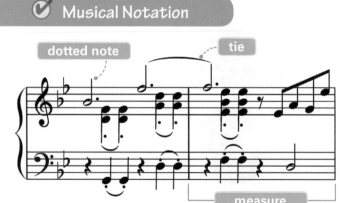

dotted note

tie

measure

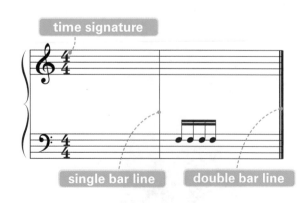

time signature

single bar line

double bar line

Main Idea and Details

1   What is the passage mainly about?

   a. How to read musical notation.   **b.** Why musical notation is popular.

   c. What a tie and dotted note are.

2   The time signature shows the _____ of the music.

   a. tie   **b.** beat   **c.** dot

3   What does a double bar line show?

   a. Where a piece of music ends.   **b.** Where a measure begins and ends.

   c. What the length of the music is.

4   What does rhythm mean?

   a. Time.   **b.** Pitch.   **c.** Tempo.

5   According to the passage, which statement is true?

   a. It is very difficult to learn musical notation.

   b. Musical notes tell the rhythm and the beat of the piece.

   c. People around the world can read music thanks to musical notation.

6   Complete the outline.

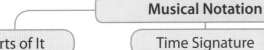

Musical Notation		
Parts of It	**Time Signature**	**Measure**
• Note = tells the rhythm, length, and ᵃ_____ of the music • Dotted note = should be increased by half • ᵇ_____ = a curved line connecting the notes	• Is at the beginning of a piece of music • Shows the ᶜ_____ or beat of the piece • Could be $\frac{4}{4}$, $\frac{3}{4}$, or $\frac{2}{4}$	• Is a division of music • ᵈ_____ _____ _____ = shows where a measure begins and ends • Double bar line = shows where a piece of music ends

Vocabulary Builder

Write the correct word and the meaning in Chinese.

1  ▸ a way to write down music

_____

2 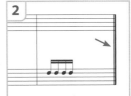 ▸ a line used to show where a piece of music is finished

_____

3  ▸ a curved line that joins two musical notes of the same pitch to denote a single tone sustained through the time value of the two

_____

4  ▸ a division of music; the unit of music contained between two bar lines

_____

Key Words

- outstanding
- organist
- Baroque Period
- concerto
- cantata
- choral music
- lyrics
- composition
- orchestra
- symphony

There have been many outstanding composers of classical music. Three of them are Johann Sebastian Bach, George Friedrich Handel, and Joseph Haydn.

Bach was a German composer and organist from the Baroque Period. He composed numerous works of music, including organ music, concertos, cantatas, and a lot of choral music for the church. The *Brandenburg Concertos* and *St. Matthew Passion* are some of his best-known works.

Johann Sebastian Bach

George Friedrich Handel

Handel was another German Baroque composer. However, Handel mostly lived in England and composed music with English lyrics. Handel is best known for his compositions based on stories from the Bible. The famous *Messiah*, which is performed by an orchestra and a chorus, is one of these pieces. It includes the *Hallelujah Chorus*, one of the most popular works in all classical music.

Joseph Haydn

Haydn lived after Bach and Handel during the Classical Period. He is sometimes called the Father of the Symphony. He composed more than one hundred symphonies. *The Surprise Symphony* and *The Creation* are his best-known symphonies. People also remember him for being the teacher of Ludwig van Beethoven, one of the greatest of all classical composers.

Main Idea and Details

1 **What is the passage mainly about?**

a. The teachers of Ludwig van Beethoven.   **b.** The greatest of all composers.

c. Some outstanding classical music composers.

2 **Joseph Haydn composed** _____.

a. *The Creation*   **b.** the *Hallelujah Chorus*

c. the *Brandenburg Concertos*

3 **What language did Handel compose his works in?**

a. English.   **b.** German.   **c.** French.

4 **What does performed mean?**

a. Written.   **b.** Practiced.   **c.** Played.

5 **Complete the sentences.**

a. Both Bach and Handel lived during the _____ Period.

b. Many of the works of _____ were based on stories from the Bible.

c. _____ is called the Father of the Symphony.

6 **Complete the outline.**

Classical Music Composers

Johann Sebastian Bach
- Lived in the ᵃ_____ Period
- Composed organ music, concertos, cantatas, and choral music

George Friedrich Handel
- Was a German Baroque composer
- Wrote ᵇ_____ in English
- Composed works based on ᶜ_____ stories

Joseph Haydn
- Lived in the ᵈ_____ Period
- Is called the Father of the ᵉ_____
- Taught Ludwig van Beethoven

Vocabulary Builder

Write the correct word and the meaning in Chinese.

1  ▸ the words of a song

_____

2  ▸ a piece of religious music performed by singers and an orchestra

_____

3  ▸ a long piece of classical music played by an orchestra

_____

4  ▸ something composed; a piece of music

_____

Vocabulary Review 9

A Complete the sentences with the words below.

minaret	collapsing	medieval	copied
statues	cathedrals	Muslims	carved

1 Many Gothic _____ had towers and spires that reached high in the air.

2 Because the cathedrals were so tall and enormous, buttresses supported the cathedrals and kept them from _____.

3 Some of the most beautiful _____ art is found in books called illuminated manuscripts.

4 During the Middle Ages, books were _____ by hand by monks.

5 During the Middle Ages, _____ developed a very different architecture style from the Gothic style.

6 One of the main features of Islamic architecture is the _____.

7 In Africa, artists made both _____ and masks.

8 To remember their ancestors, African people _____ sculptures and made many masks.

B Complete the sentences with the words below.

time signature	symphonies	Baroque	notes
songwriters	outstanding	measures	Bible

1 _____ and composers use a special kind of writing called "notation" to write down their music.

2 The _____ basically tell us the rhythm, length, and pitch of the music.

3 At the beginning of each piece of music is the _____ _____.

4 Composers often divide their music into _____.

5 There have been many _____ composers of classical music.

6 Bach was a German composer and organist from the _____ Period.

7 Handel is best known for his compositions based on stories from the _____.

8 Haydn composed more than one hundred _____.

C Write the correct word and the meaning in Chinese.

1 ▸ a stone brace that supports a cathedral so that it does not collapse

_____

2 ▸ an evil spirit

_____

3 ▸ a tall tower found at each of the four corners of a mosque

_____

4 ▸ something composed; a piece of music

_____

5 ▸ a symbol that indicates that a note should be increased by half

_____

6 ▸ meter signature

_____

D Match each word with the correct definition and write the meaning in Chinese.

1 inspire _____ ☐

2 awe-inspiring _____ ☐

3 musical notation _____ ☐

4 depict _____ ☐

5 mosque _____ ☐

6 measure _____ ☐

7 outstanding _____ ☐

8 numerous _____ ☐

9 choral music _____ ☐

10 composition _____ ☐

a. very many

b. a choir or chorus

c. making one feel awe

d. very remarkable; excellent

e. a way to write down music

f. a Muslim place of worship

g. something composed; a piece of music

h. to encourage someone to do something good

i. a division of music; the unit of music contained between two bar lines

j. to show something through a painting or sculpture

Wrap-Up Test **3**

A

Write the correct word for each sentence.

| denominators | compound | numerator | tense | cathedrals |
| acute angle | incomplete | diameter | prefixes | notation |

1. A common factor is a number that the _____ and denominator can both be divided by.

2. To compare unlike fractions, you need to make their _____ the same.

3. An _____ _____ measures greater than 0° and less than 90°.

4. The _____ is a chord that bisects a circle.

5. _____ and suffixes are groups of letters that are added to the fronts or ends of words.

6. A _____ sentence contains two or more complete sentences.

7. The _____ shows the time in which an action takes place.

8. A sentence fragment is a part of a sentence or an _____ sentence.

9. During the Middle Ages, many magnificent Gothic _____ were built in Europe.

10. Once you can read the _____, you can freely sing and play music.

B

Write the meanings of the words in Chinese.

1. improper fraction _____
2. equivalent fraction _____
3. ray _____
4. protractor _____
5. parallelogram _____
6. radius _____
7. common factor _____
8. simplest form _____
9. common denominator _____
10. unlike fractions _____
11. obtuse angle _____
12. isosceles triangle _____
13. diameter _____
14. suffix _____
15. sentence fragment _____

16. conjunction _____
17. proofreading mark _____
18. amusement park _____
19. break down _____
20. take place _____
21. predicate _____
22. compound sentence _____
23. insert _____
24. medieval _____
25. buttress _____
26. minaret _____
27. time signature _____
28. awe-inspiring _____
29. musical notation _____
30. composition _____

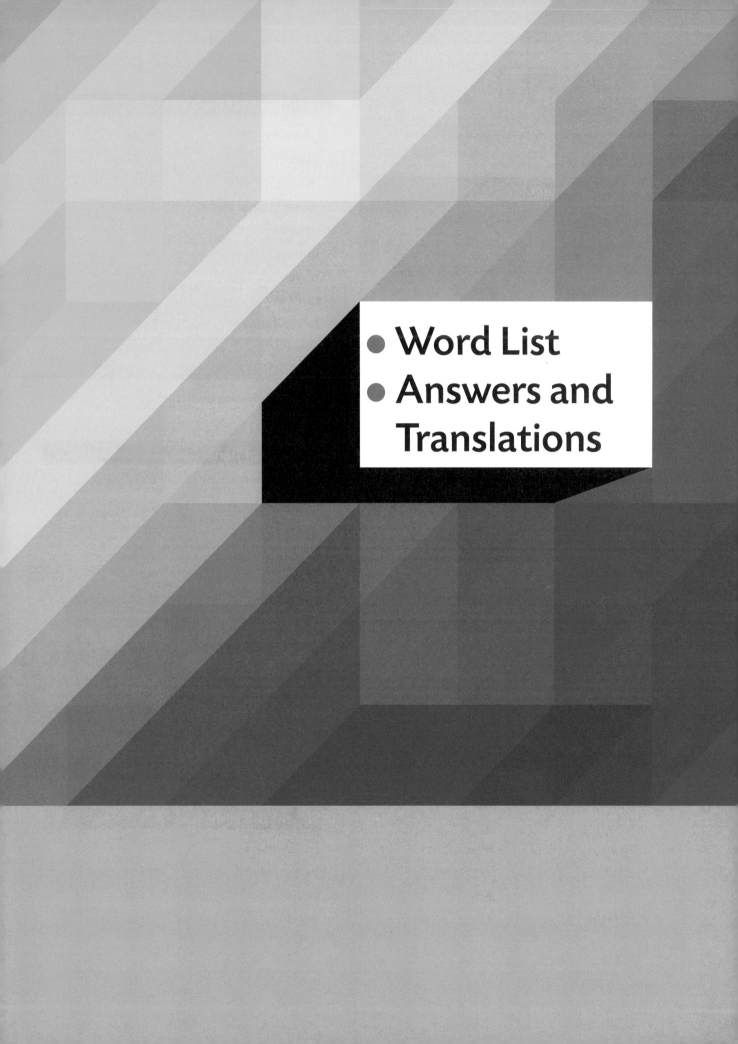

- Word List
- Answers and Translations

Word List

01 Reading Maps

1	**political map**	行政區域圖
2	**territorial** (a.)	領土的
3	**border** (n.)	邊界
4	**physical map**	自然地圖
5	**landform** (n.)	地形
6	**body of water**	水域
7	**rely on**	依賴
8	**display** (v.)	顯示
9	**geographical** (a.)	地理的
10	**feature** (n.)	特徵
11	**historical map**	歷史地圖
12	**road map**	道路地圖
13	**focus on**	專注於
14	**route** (n.)	路線
15	**set onto**	設置在……之上
16	**locator / locator map**	定位圖；定位地圖

02 Mountains, Rivers, and Deserts of the World

1	**steep** (a.)	陡峭的
2	**side** (n.)	側面；斜坡
3	**mountain range**	山脈
4	**mountain chain**	山脈
5	**peak** (n.)	山峰
6	**source** (n.)	源頭；水源
7	**tributary** (n.)	支流
8	**empty into**	流入
9	**mighty** (a.)	巨大的；浩瀚的
10	**rainfall** (n.)	降雨；降雨量
11	**arid** (a.)	乾燥的
12	**Antarctica** (n.)	南極洲

03 A World of Trade

1	**globalize** (v.)	全球化
2	**planet** (n.)	地球；行星
3	**in contact with**	與……聯繫
4	**international trade**	國際貿易
5	**export** (v.)	出口
6	**import** (v.)	進口
7	**buyer** (n.)	購買者
8	**tariff** (n.)	關稅
9	**interference** (n.)	干涉
10	**free trade**	自由貿易
11	**free market economy**	自由市場經濟
12	**control** (v.)	控制

04 Ancient Trade

1	**benefit** (v.)	受益；受惠
2	**human resources**	人力資源
3	**item** (n.)	物品
4	**thanks to**	由於
5	**communication** (n.)	通訊
6	**cargo ship**	貨船
7	**conduct** (v.)	進行
8	**Mediterranean Sea**	地中海
9	**pottery** (n.)	陶器
10	**barter** (v.)	以……作為交換；拿……來以物易物
11	**merchant** (n.)	商人
12	**spice** (n.)	香料

05 The Gift of the Nile

1	**civilization** (n.)	文明
2	**be centered on**	集中於
3	**fertile** (a.)	肥沃的
4	**flood** (v.)	氾濫
5	**topsoil** (n.)	表土

6	silt (n.)	淤泥
7	population (n.)	人口
8	pharaoh (n.)	法老（古埃及國王）
9	be descended from	是……的後裔
10	construct (v.)	建造
11	temple (n.)	（古希臘、羅馬、埃及的）神殿
12	monument (n.)	紀念碑
13	hieroglyphics (n.)	象形文字
14	be carved on	被雕刻於……

06 The Culture of Egypt

1	worship (v.)	信奉
2	appearance (n.)	外貌
3	falcon (n.)	隼；獵鷹
4	jackal (n.)	豺狼；胡狼
5	chaos (n.)	混亂
6	the underworld	陰間
7	fertility (n.)	生育力
8	kingdom (n.)	王國
9	prosperous (a.)	繁榮的
10	reign (n.)	統治時期
11	preserve (v.)	保存
12	the dead	死者
13	mummy (n.)	木乃伊

07 Ancient Greece

1	brilliant (a.)	輝煌的
2	city-state (n.)	（古希臘的）城邦
3	acropolis (n.)	（古希臘城市的）衛城
4	walled (a.)	有圍牆的；有城牆的
5	seek (v.)	尋求 * 動詞三態 seek-sought-sought
6	unite (v.)	團結
7	birthplace (n.)	出生地；發源地
8	take part in	參與……
9	warrior (n.)	戰士

10	train (v.)	訓練
11	compete (v.)	競賽
12	Peloponnesian War	伯羅奔尼撒戰爭
13	defeat (v.)	擊敗
14	general (n.)	將軍

08 Socrates and Plato

1	thinker (n.)	思想家
2	political science	政治學
3	a series of	一連串的；一系列的
4	be designed to	目的是……
5	questioner (n.)	發問者
6	annoy (v.)	使惱怒
7	trial (n.)	審判
8	urge (v.)	煽動
9	revolt (v.)	反叛
10	guilty (a.)	有罪的
11	be sentenced to death	被處死刑
12	involve (v.)	牽涉
13	ideal (a.)	理想的
14	found (v.)	建立

09 Ancient Rome

1	peninsula (n.)	半島
2	neighboring (a.)	鄰近的
3	drive out	驅逐
4	republic (n.)	共和政體
5	elect (v.)	選舉
6	consul (n.)	執政官
7	Senate (n.)	元老院
8	landowner (n.)	地主
9	class (n.)	階級
10	patrician (n.)	貴族
11	plebeian (n.)	平民
12	Punic War	布匿戰爭
13	Carthage (n.)	迦太基
14	rival (a.)	競爭的

10　The Founding of Rome

1	legend (n.)	傳說
2	found (v.)	建立
3	priestess (n.)	女祭司
4	overthrow (v.)	推翻 * 動詞三態 overthrow- overthrew-overthrown
5	be thrown into	被丟入……
6	fear (v.)	害怕
7	rescue (v.)	援救
8	as if	猶如
9	shepherd (n.)	牧羊人
10	raise (v.)	養育
11	argue (v.)	爭吵
12	terrible (a.)	嚴重的
13	argument (n.)	爭執
14	name after	以……的名字命名

11　Europe in the Middle Ages

1	collapse (v.)	瓦解
2	split (v.)	分裂 * 動詞三態 split-split-split
3	Germanic (a.)	日耳曼民族的
4	invader (n.)	侵略者
5	Byzantine Empire	拜占庭帝國
6	official (a.)	法定的；正式的
7	Emperor Constantine	君士坦丁大帝
8	Charlemagne (n.)	查理曼大帝
9	troops (n.)	軍隊（作複數形）
10	eventually (adv.)	最後

12　Feudalism

1	feudalism (n.)	封建制度
2	practice (v.)	實行
3	fief (n.)	采邑；封地
4	lord (n.)	領主
5	vassal (n.)	附庸；封臣
6	faithfully (adv.)	忠實地
7	swear (v.)	宣誓 * 動詞三態 swear-swore-sworn
8	oath (n.)	誓言
9	knight (n.)	騎士
10	armor (n.)	盔甲
11	on horseback	騎著馬的；在馬背上的
12	serf (n.)	農奴
13	peasant (n.)	僱農
14	manor (n.)	莊園；莊園大屋
15	move away	離開
16	permission (n.)	准許

13　What Is the Scientific Method?

1	curious (a.)	好奇的
2	inquiry (n.)	詢問；質詢
3	scientific method	科學方法
4	figure out	想出（答案等）
5	observation (n.)	觀察
6	observe (v.)	觀察
7	basis (n.)	基礎；準則
8	hypothesis (n.)	假設
9	make a prediction	做出預測
10	based on	根據
11	testable (a.)	可驗證的
12	experiment (n.)	實驗
13	collect (v.)	收集
14	interpret (v.)	解釋；說明
15	draw a conclusion	下結論
16	support (v.)	支持

14　Scientific Tools

1	laboratory (n.)	實驗室
2	be filled with	充滿

3	manipulate (v.)	操作
4	measuring cup	量杯
5	graduated cylinder	量筒
6	magnifying glass	放大鏡
7	handheld (a.)	手持的
8	microscope (n.)	顯微鏡
9	magnify (v.)	放大
10	forceps (n.)	鑷子
11	extremely (adv.)	極端地
12	lab coat	實驗服

15 What Are Cells?

1	unit (n.)	單位
2	cell (n.)	細胞
3	nucleus (n.)	細胞核
4	outer (a.)	外面的
5	covering (n.)	覆蓋物
6	cell membrane	細胞膜
7	cytoplasm (n.)	細胞質
8	cell wall	細胞壁
9	stiff (a.)	硬的
10	chloroplast (n.)	葉綠體
11	chlorophyll (n.)	葉綠素
12	photosynthesis (n.)	光合作用
13	specialized (a.)	專門的
14	tissue (n.)	（動植物的）組織
15	organ (n.)	器官
16	kidney (n.)	腎臟

16 Classifying Living Things

1	be formed of	由……構成
2	human (n.)	人類
3	be made up of	由……組成
4	in common	共同的；共有的
5	classify (v.)	將……分類
6	compare (v.)	比較

7	one-celled (a.)	單細胞的
8	multi-celled (a.)	多細胞的
9	microorganism (n.)	微生物
10	microscopic (a.)	微小的；用顯微鏡才能看見的
11	protist (n.)	原生生物
12	fungus (n.)	真菌；菌類植物 * pl. fungi

17 What Is Heredity?

1	wonder (v.)	對……感到疑惑；想知道
2	look like	看起來像……
3	perhaps (adv.)	或許
4	similar-looking (a.)	看起來相似的
5	similarity (n.)	相似點
6	heredity (n.)	遺傳
7	pass down	傳下來
8	trait (n.)	特徵
9	offspring (n.)	後代；子女
10	gene (n.)	基因
11	instruction (n.)	指示
12	vary (v.)	變化
13	sperm cell	精細胞
14	egg cell	卵細胞
15	genetic (a.)	基因的；遺傳的
16	inherit (v.)	經遺傳而獲得（性格、特徵等）
17	dominant gene	顯性基因
18	recessive gene	隱性基因

18 What Are Traits?

1	trait (n.)	特徵
2	characteristic (n.)	特性
3	affect (v.)	影響
4	combination (n.)	結合
5	nurture (n.) (v.)	養育；教養
6	inherited trait	遺傳特徵
7	learned trait	習得特徵
8	alter (v.)	改變

9 **be determined by** 由……所決定

10 **gene's information** 基因資訊

19 The Formation of the Earth

1 **4.5 billion years** 四十五億年

2 **undergo** (v.) 經歷
* 動詞三態
undergo-underwent-undergone

3 **time period** 時期

4 **geologic** (a.) 地質學的

5 **time scale** 時間表；年代表

6 **era** (n.) 時代；【地】代

7 **Precambrian Era** 前寒武紀時代

8 **comprise** (v.) 包含

9 **Paleozoic Era** 古生代

10 **stabilize** (v.) 穩定

11 **invertebrate** (n.) 無脊椎動物

12 **evolve** (v.) 演化；進化

13 **Mesozoic Era** 中生代

14 **dominate** (v.) 主宰

15 **Cenozoic Era** 新生代

16 **refer to . . . as . . .** 稱……為……

20 Continental Drift

1 **supercontinent** (n.) 超大陸

2 **assume** (v.) 假定

3 **pull apart** 拉開；拆開

4 **mystery** (n.) 謎

5 **theory** (n.) 學說；理論

6 **continental drift** 大陸漂移

7 **crust** (n.) 地殼

8 **plate** (n.) 板塊

9 **mantle** (n.) 地函

10 **melted rock** 熔岩

11 **constantly** (adv.) 不斷地

12 **continually** (adv.) 持續地

21 Light and Heat

1 **light wave** 光波

2 **reflect** (v.) 反射

3 **refract** (v.) 折射

4 **bounce off** 反射；彈回

5 **reflection** (n.) 反射

6 **refraction** (n.) 折射

7 **bend** (v.) 彎曲
* 動詞三態
bend-bent-bent

8 **conduction** (n.) 傳導

9 **convection** (n.) 對流

10 **radiation** (n.) 輻射

11 **conduct** (v.) 傳導

12 **heated** (a.) 加熱的；受熱的

22 Electricity

1 **static electricity** 靜電

2 **current electricity** 電流

3 **electric charge** 電荷

4 **temporary** (a.) 短暫的

5 **unpredictable** (a.) 不可預測的

6 **steady** (a.) 穩定的

7 **bulb** (n.) 電燈泡

8 **electric circuit** 電路

9 **electric current** 電流

10 **link** (v.) 連接

11 **closed circuit** 閉合電路；閉路

12 **open circuit** 開路；斷路

13 **series circuit** 串聯電路

14 **parallel circuit** 並聯電路

23 Motion and Force

1 **velocity** (n.) 速度

2 **rate of speed** 速率

3 **position** (n.) 位置

4	**force** (n.)	力
5	**law of inertia**	慣性定律
6	**gravity** (n.)	地心引力
7	**gravitation** (n.)	萬有引力
8	**orbit** (n.)	軌道
9	**friction** (n.)	摩擦力
10	**rub** (v.)	摩擦

24 Simple Machines

1	**device** (n.)	裝置
2	**complex** (a.)	複雜的
3	**inclined plane**	斜面
4	**ramp** (n.)	斜面；斜坡
5	**wedge** (n.)	楔子
6	**back to back**	背對背
7	**screw** (n.)	螺旋
8	**lever** (n.)	槓桿
9	**apply** (v.)	使用；施用
10	**pliers** (n.)	鉗子
11	**pulley** (n.)	滑輪
12	**grooved** (a.)	表面有溝槽的
13	**rim** (n.)	框邊
14	**wheel and axle**	輪軸
15	**post** (n.)	桿子
16	**axle** (n.)	軸
17	**turning force**	轉力
18	**doorknob** (n.)	球形門把
19	**screwdriver** (n.)	螺絲起子

25 Understanding Fractions

1	**name** (v.)	陳述
2	**equal part**	等分
3	**unit fraction**	單位分數
4	**numerator** (n.)	分子
5	**denominator** (n.)	分母
6	**improper fraction**	假分數

7	**whole number**	整數
8	**mixed number**	帶分數
9	**division sign**	除號
10	**equivalent fraction**	等值分數
11	**common factor**	公因數
12	**simplest form**	最簡分數

26 Word Problems With Fractions

1	**greatest common factor**	最大公因數
2	**solution** (n.)	解答
3	**reduce** (v.)	約分
4	**in one step**	一步到位
5	**common denominator**	公分母
6	**unlike fractions**	異分母分數

27 Lines and Angles

1	**line segment**	線段
2	**ray** (n.)	射線
3	**angle** (n.)	角
4	**vertex** (n.)	頂點
5	**degree** (n.)	度
6	**protractor** (n.)	量角器
7	**right angle**	直角
8	**perpendicular line**	垂直線
9	**intersect** (v.)	相交
10	**acute angle**	銳角
11	**obtuse angle**	鈍角
12	**straight angle**	平角

28 Polygons, Triangles, and Circles

1	**polygon** (n.)	多邊形
2	**closed figure**	封閉圖形
3	**side** (n.)	邊
4	**parallelogram** (n.)	平行四邊形
5	**rhombus** (n.)	菱形
6	**trapezoid** (n.)	梯形

7 **pentagon** (n.) 五邊形

8 **hexagon** (n.) 六邊形

9 **equilateral triangle** 等邊三角形

10 **isosceles triangle** 等腰三角形

11 **scalene triangle** 不等邊三角形

12 **chord** (n.) 弦

13 **diameter** (n.) 直徑

14 **radius** (n.) 半徑

29 Prefixes and Suffixes

1 **prefix** (n.) 字首

2 **suffix** (n.) 字尾

3 **extra** (a.) 額外的

4 **among** (prep.) 在……之中

5 **independent** (a.) 獨立的

6 **preview** (n.) (v.) 預習

7 **foreground** (n.) 前景

8 **midterm** (n.) 期中考

9 **past tense form** 過去式

10 **continuous form** 進行式

11 **break down** 分解

12 **root** (n.) 字根

30 Tenses

1 **tense** (n.) 時態

2 **take place** 發生

3 **past tense** 過去式

4 **present tense** 現在式

5 **future tense** 未來式

6 **describe** (v.) 描述

7 **repeated** (a.) 重複的；反覆的

8 **habitual** (a.) 習慣的

9 **continuous tense** 進行式

10 **perfect tense** 完成式

31 Complete Sentences

1 **complete sentence** 完整句

2 **subject** (n.) 主詞

3 **predicate** (n.) 述語

4 **pronoun** (n.) 代名詞

5 **part of speech** 詞性

6 **sentence fragment** 句子片斷；不完整句

7 **miss** (v.) 遺漏

8 **compound sentence** 複合句

9 **conjunction** (n.) 連接詞

10 **run-on sentence** 連寫句；不斷句

32 Proofreading

1 **paragraph** (n.) （文章的）段

2 **mistake** (n.) 錯誤

3 **proofread** (v.) 校對
　　* 動詞三態　proofread-
　　proofread-proofread

4 **proofreading mark** 校對符號

5 **incorrect** (a.) 不正確的

6 **insert** (v.) 插入

7 **punctuation** (n.) 標點符號

8 **delete** (v.) 刪除

9 **capitalize** (v.) 用大寫書寫

10 **lowercase** (v.) 用小寫書寫

11 **amusement park** 遊樂園

12 **wait in line** 排隊

13 **get tired** 疲倦

14 **get crowded** 人潮擁擠

33 The Art of the Middle Ages

1 **Middle Ages** 中世紀

2 **magnificent** (a.) 雄偉的

3 **Gothic** (a.) 哥德式的

4 **cathedral** (n.) 大教堂

5 **spire** (n.) 尖塔

6	inspire (v.)	激起；喚起
7	awe-inspiring (a.)	令人肅然起敬的
8	buttress (n.)	扶壁
9	demon (n.)	惡魔
10	gargoyle (n.)	滴水獸
11	medieval (a.)	中世紀的
12	illuminated (a.)	（書籍等）用鮮明圖案裝飾的
13	manuscript (n.)	手抄本；手稿
14	monk (n.)	僧侶
15	a bit of / bits of	少許……；一些……

34 The Art of Islam and Africa

1	Muslim (n.)	穆斯林；伊斯蘭教徒
2	architecture (n.)	建築
3	mosque (n.)	清真寺
4	minaret (n.)	喚拜塔；叫拜樓（清真寺的尖塔）
5	statue (n.)	雕像
6	ancestor (n.)	祖先
7	typically (adv.)	典型地
8	terra cotta	赤陶土
9	brass (n.)	黃銅
10	mask dance	面具舞
11	depict (v.)	描繪

35 Musical Notation

1	no matter what	無論什麼
2	read music	讀樂譜
3	musical notation	樂譜
4	songwriter (n.)	詞曲創作人
5	composer (n.)	作曲家
6	staff (n.)	五線譜
7	dotted note	附點音符
8	tie (n.)	連結線
9	time signature	拍號
10	measure (n.)	小節
11	meter (n.)	節拍
12	double bar line	雙小節線

36 Composers and Their Music

1	outstanding (a.)	傑出的
2	numerous (a.)	為數眾多的
3	choral music	合唱音樂
4	best-known (a.)	最著名的
5	lyrics (n.)	歌詞（作複數形）
6	composition (n.)	樂曲
7	based on	根據
8	chorus (n.)	合唱團

01 Reading Maps 看地圖

地圖有很多種類。

「行政區域圖」顯示各個城市、州和國家的地理位置。這種地圖以線條來標示領土邊界，例如州界和國界。

「自然地圖」顯示地形和水域。地形是地表上的各種陸地型態。水域則包含海洋、河川和湖泊。這些地圖運用顏色來表現不同的地理特徵，例如，藍色代表水域，褐色代表山脈，綠色代表森林。自然地圖也叫做「地形圖」。

「歷史地圖」是顯示過去事件及其發生地點相關資訊的地圖。這種地圖的標題通常包含日期。

「道路圖」和「交通路線圖」著重於街道，它們會標示重要的建築物與交通路線，例如機場、鐵路和高速公路。

有時你會看到主圖上面附有一個小地圖，我們稱之為「定位圖」或「定位地圖」，用來顯示主要地圖所在的地區。

- **Main Idea and Details**
1 (b)　　2 (a)　　3 (b)　　4 (b)
5 a. **borders**　b. **historical**　c. **highways**
6 a. **lines**　b. **geographical**　c. **events**
　d. **transportation**　e. **main map**

- **Vocabulary Builder**
1 **territorial** 領土的
2 **border** 邊界
3 **focus on** 集中於（焦點）
4 **locator / locator map** 定位圖／定位地圖

02 Mountains, Rivers, and Deserts of the World 全球的山脈、河流和沙漠

山是具有陡坡的高聳地形，經常構成山脈或山系。喜馬拉雅山脈位於亞洲，世界最高峰聖母峰和許多其他高峰都位於此山脈。歐洲則有阿爾卑斯山脈；南美洲有安地斯山脈；北美洲有阿帕拉契山脈和落磯山脈。

河是流入其他水域的長條水流。河的源頭——也就是河流起源處——可能位於山中的高處，接著它們會流入海洋。許多支流也會流入大河內。世界最長的河流是非洲的尼羅河，南美洲的亞馬遜河也是一條幅員廣闊的河流，而美國的密西西比河則有「浩瀚的密西西比」之稱。

沙漠是動植物稀少的極乾燥陸地，這裡的雨量非常稀少，因此多半炎熱而乾燥。然而也有寒冷的沙漠，南極洲就是一個寒漠。全世界最大的沙漠是非洲的撒哈拉沙漠，第二大是中東的阿拉伯沙漠，亞洲的戈壁沙漠也是一座廣大的沙漠。

- **Main Idea and Details**
1 (c)　　2 (c)　　3 (b)　　4 (b)　　5 (c)
6 a. **Asia**　b. **Rocky Mountains**　c. **streams**　d. **mighty**
　e. **Sahara**

- **Vocabulary Builder**
1 **mighty** 強大的；浩瀚的
2 **source**（河的）源頭
3 **tributary** 支流
4 **arid** 乾燥的

03 A World of Trade 貿易的世界

我們居住在全球化的世界，這表示地球上的每個區域都能彼此聯繫。人們互相聯繫的一種方式是透過貿易，而貿易就是商品和服務的買賣。

不同國家之間的貿易稱為國際貿易。許多企業會試著將商品銷售到世界各地，當它們把商品運送到別的國家，就是在「出口」這些商品；許多企業也會向別的國家購買原料和其他產品，當它們向外國購買商品，就是在「進口」這些商品。而多數國家會試著讓出口量大於進口量。

通常，商品進口時，買方必須支付關稅。關稅是國家對進口貨物所徵收的稅。無須課稅或不受政府干預的貿易，則稱為自由貿易。

世界上許多國家擁有自由市場經濟，在自由市場經濟之下，要生產和購買何種產品由人民自行決定。然而，在某些國家中，買賣的產品則是由政府掌控。

- **Main Idea and Details**
1 (c)　　2 (c)　　3 (b)　　4 (c)
5 a. **Trade is the buying and selling of goods and services.**
　b. **International trade is trade between different countries.**
　c. **Free trade is trade that has no taxes or government interference.**
6 a. **selling**　b. **countries**　c. **bring**　d. **tax**

- **Vocabulary Builder**
1 **export** 出口
2 **globalize** 使全球化
3 **free trade** 自由貿易
4 **interference** 干涉

04 Ancient Trade 古代貿易

人們為什麼要交易？人們互相交易是因為可以雙雙獲利。世界各國擁有不同的自然資源和人力資源，每個國家的人們也使用這些資源生產不同的商品。他們用這些商品交換自己沒有生產的貨物時，就是所謂的「貿易」。

由於交通運輸工具和通訊設備的發明，今日世界各地的人們相較於過去，能夠更快速地進行貿易。

很久以前，人類也有貿易的行為。數千年前還沒有貨船、飛機、電話或電腦，但是人們依然能夠進行國與國之間的貿易。

舉例來說，古希臘人曾經在地中海周邊進行貿易，他們除了生產精美的陶器，也種植橄欖和葡萄，並以這些產品交換所需的物品。希臘的船隻經常越洋航行到埃及，並於當地用他們的產品交換棉花、水果和小麥。

古羅馬人也會和埃及與其他鄰近國家交易，他們也跟中國和印度交易。當時的商人經由名為「絲路」的路線前往中國，用黃金和農產品交換中國與印度的絲綢、寶石和香料。

- Main Idea and Details

1 (a)　　2 (b)　　3 (a)　　4 (c)
5 a. quickly　　b. Silk Road　　c. India
6 a. Mediterranean　b. cotton　c. China　d. gems

- Vocabulary Builder

1 pottery 陶器　　　　　2 Silk Road 絲路
3 merchant 商人　　　　4 spice 香料

Vocabulary Review 1

A
1 territorial　　　　　2 physical
3 transportation　　　4 locator
5 landforms　　　　　6 peaks
7 streams　　　　　　8 rainfall
B
1 selling　　　　　　2 imported
3 tariff　　　　　　　4 free market
5 benefit　　　　　　6 communication
7 Mediterranean　　　8 Silk Road
C
1 mountain range/chain 山脈
2 route 路線
3 locator / locator map 定位圖；定位地圖
4 cargo ship 貨船
5 human resources 人力資
6 barter 以……交換……；以物易物
D
1 地形 j　　　　　　2 邊界 i
3 陡峭的 d　　　　　4 支流 g
5 乾燥的 a　　　　　6 出口 f
7 進口 h　　　　　　8 關稅 c
9 干涉 b　　　　　　10 以……交換…… e

05 The Gift of the Nile 尼羅河的恩賜

最早的人類文明之一於五千年前形成於埃及，集中在尼羅河沿岸。尼羅河每年定期氾濫，因此周圍的土壤十分肥沃。河水氾濫期間，在陸地上留下肥沃的表土和淤泥，讓農人得以種植大量農作物。沒多久，埃及就聚集了大量的人口。

古埃及由法老王所統治。法老是國王，但人民相信法老是神的後裔。法老被視為神王，統治身為奴隸的埃及人。

古埃及人是偉大的工程師和建築師，他們建造出雄偉的金字塔，來作為法老的墳墓。他們同時也在金字塔附近建造了獅身人面像，並在埃及境內修建了許多其他的石造神殿和紀念碑。

古埃及人發展出一套叫做「象形文字」的書寫系統，這套系統運用了代表概念、聲音和物體的圖畫和符號。象形文字被刻於牆壁和紀念碑上。

- Main Idea and Details

1 (c)　　2 (b)　　3 (a)　　4 (c)　　5 (c)
6 a. fertile　b. population　c. god-kings　d. symbols

- Vocabulary Builder

1 pharaoh 法老（古埃及國王）　2 the Sphinx 獅身人面像
3 monument 紀念碑　　　　　　4 hieroglyphics 象形文字

06 The Culture of Egypt 埃及文化

古埃及人信奉許多神祇，這些神祇通常兼具人與動物的外貌。其中最重要的神是太陽神「拉」，祂有著鷹頭，古埃及人相信法老即為「拉」之子。另一位太陽神荷魯斯也是鷹首人身。阿努比斯是死神，有著一顆胡狼頭。賽特是混亂之神。歐西里斯統治陰間。伊西絲是歐西里斯的姊妹兼妻子，也是荷魯斯的母親，祂是生育女神，同時保護著人民遠離病痛和傷害。

埃及的法老既有財富又有權勢。美尼斯統一了兩個王國，成為埃及的第一位法老。拉美西斯二世是所有法老中最偉大、權勢最大的一位，曾征服了許多領土。而在阿蒙霍特普三世統治下的埃及則是最繁榮的時期。

古埃及人相信人死後能夠重生，因此埃及文化集中於死者的來生。他們發展出一套保存死者的方式，將屍體製成木乃伊。同時，埃及的陵墓也保存了一個人在來世所需的一切物品。

- Main Idea and Details

1 (c)　　2 (c)　　3 (a)　　4 (b)
5 a. Ra and Horus had the head of a falcon.
　b. Menes was the first pharaoh of Egypt.
　c. A mummy was a dead body which was wrapped in cloth and preserved long ago.
6 a. dead　b. fertility　c. Ramses II　d. death　e. next lives

- Vocabulary Builder

1 jackal 胡狼；豺狼　　　　2 chaos 混亂
3 reign 統治；統治期間　　　4 mummy 木乃伊

07 Ancient Greece 古希臘

最輝煌的古文明之一出現在希臘。希臘人居住在許多不同的城邦中，大多數的城邦圍繞著衛城而建立，而衛城則是築有圍牆的山丘，人民靠著衛城得以躲避攻擊。各個城邦經常彼此征戰，然而當面臨外敵如波斯人的侵略時，他們會團結起來聯手抵抗外侮。

雅典和斯巴達是古希臘最強盛的兩個城邦，兩者擁有截然不同的價值觀與文化。

雅典是民主的發源地。雅典的公民有投票權和參政權，但是只有成年男子才能成為公民。斯巴達人非常強悍，是偉大的戰士。斯巴達的男孩從小被訓練成為戰士，甚至女子也被訓練參加體育競賽。雅典和斯巴達在伯羅奔尼撒戰爭之中對戰，最終斯巴達擊敗了雅典。

希臘孕育出許多偉大的藝術家、科學家、哲學家、政治家乃至將軍。然而，在西元前四世紀時，亞歷山大大帝征服了希臘各城邦，並將它們納入其帝國版圖內。

- **Main Idea and Details**

1 (c)　　2 (a)　　3 (c)　　4 (c)

5 a. **unite**　　b. **soldiers**　　c. **Alexander the Great**

6 a. **foreign**　b. **democracy**　c. **government**　d. **Peloponnesian**

- **Vocabulary Builder**

1 **democracy** 民主；民主政體

2 **acropolis**（古希臘城市的）衛城

3 **philosopher** 哲學家　　　　4 **defeat** 擊敗

08 Socrates and Plato 蘇格拉底和柏拉圖

古希臘孕育出許多偉大的思想家和哲學家。希臘哲學家研究歷史、政治學乃至數學，通常也會教導學生。而古希臘最偉大的兩位哲人就是蘇格拉底和柏拉圖。

蘇格拉底是一位雅典的導師，主持關於生活方式的討論。他使用一種被稱為「蘇格拉底法」的詰問形式，基本上，他會提出一連串的問題，這些問題的目的是為了探究某個疑難的答案，或者這些問題會表現出提問者本人（如蘇格拉底）的無知程度。

當蘇格拉底開始質詢雅典的法律、習俗和宗教時，此舉激怒了許多雅典的當政者。他被控「教唆雅典年輕人造反」而受審，判處有罪並處以死刑。

蘇格拉底吸引了無數學生，其中一位即為柏拉圖。柏拉圖記錄了蘇格拉底的所有思想，著有眾多不同的書籍，大部分是關於蘇格拉底和其他知名雅典人物的對話。其中最著名的就是《理想國》，書中描述了柏拉圖心中理想的政府形式。柏拉圖的作品非常重要，所有西方哲學的建立都受其啟發。

- **Main Idea and Details**

1 (c)　　2 (c)　　3 (b)　　4 (b)　　5 (a)

6 a. **Method**　b. **series**　c. **government**　d. **philosophy**

- **Vocabulary Builder**

1 **trial** 審判　　　　　　　2 **revolt** 反叛

3 **annoy** 惹惱；使生氣　　　4 **found** 建立

Vocabulary Review 2

A

1 civilizations　　　　2 descended

3 tombs　　　　　　　4 writing

5 appearances　　　　6 reign

7 died　　　　　　　 8 preserve

B

1 ancient　　　　　　2 acropolis

3 city-states　　　　　4 Peloponnesian

5 philosophers　　　　6 questioning

7 put on　　　　　　　8 ideal

C

1 **pharaoh** 法老（古埃及國王）　　2 **hieroglyphics** 象形文字

3 **falcon** 隼；獵鷹　　4 **conquer** 征服；攻克

5 **acropolis**（古希臘城市的）　　6 **found** 建立
　　　　衛城

D

1 神殿 **h**　　　　　　2 紀念碑 **j**

3 混亂 **e**　　　　　　4 保存 **i**

5 輝煌的 **f**　　　　　6 出生地；發源地 **c**

7 擊敗 **d**　　　　　　8 反叛 **a**

9 理想的 **g**　　　　　10 建立 **b**

09 Ancient Rome 古羅馬

在早期的歷史裡，羅馬是一個位於義大利半島台伯河畔的小城市。隨著羅馬逐漸壯大，它的軍隊征服了許多鄰近的國家。到了西元前 250 年，羅馬已征服了大半個義大利半島。

羅馬被伊特拉斯坎國王統治了兩百五十年。在西元前 510 年，羅馬人將國王驅逐，建立了羅馬共和國。共和制是一種由人民選舉政府領導人的政體形式。

每一年，羅馬共和國會由富人選出兩名領導者，稱為執政官。任何公共事務的決定都必須經過兩名執政官的同意。羅馬人也擁有元老院，負責為執政官建言。元老院是由一群富裕的地主所組成。

羅馬共和國的公民分為兩個階級：貴族和平民。貴族是擁有許多土地的有錢人，他們可成為執政官和元老院議員。平民則是一般老百姓，而奴隸最貧窮。

西元前 264 年，羅馬與位於北非的敵對城邦迦太基之間爆發了布匿戰爭。總共發生了三次艱鉅的戰爭，但最終羅馬人在西元前 146 年擊敗迦太基。此次勝利使得羅馬成為世上最強盛的帝國，延續長達近五百年之久。

- **Main Idea and Details**

1 (c)　　2 (b)　　3 (c)　　4 (a)

5 a. **It was located on the Tiber River of the Italian peninsula.**
　b. **The Romans drove out the king and founded the Roman Republic.**
　c. **There were three Punic Wars.**

6 a. **republic**　　b. **Consuls**　　c. **Plebeians**
　d. **Carthage**　　e. **empire**

- **Vocabulary Builder**

1 **peninsula** 半島　　　　2 **consul**（古羅馬的）執政官

3 **the Senate** 元老院　　 4 **rival** 競爭的

10 The Founding of Rome 羅馬的建立

傳說中羅馬是由羅慕路斯和瑞摩斯於西元前 753 年所建立。

羅慕路斯和瑞摩斯是孿生兄弟，他們的父親並不是人類，而是是羅馬戰神馬爾斯，母親是女祭司雷亞・希爾薇亞。他們的祖父曾是國王卻遭到推翻。

羅慕路斯和瑞摩斯才剛出生，就被裝進籃子投入台伯河。因為新上任的國王阿穆利烏斯深怕男孩們有朝一日可能會推翻自己。

幸運的是，籃子漂流到河岸邊，孩子們被一隻母狼救起，並將他們視如己出般地照顧。而後，一位牧羊人帶走這兩個男孩，把他們扶養成人。

這對男孩長大之後，得知了自己的身世。他們殺死阿穆利烏斯，並讓祖父重新登基。

隨後羅慕路斯和瑞摩斯決定打造屬於自己的城市，卻為許多事務起了爭執。在一次激烈的爭吵中，羅慕路斯殺了瑞摩斯。最終羅慕路斯在台伯河畔的七座山上建立了他的城邦，並以自己的名字將這座城邦命名為羅馬。

- **Main Idea and Details**

1 **(c)**　　2 **(c)**　　3 **(a)**　　4 **(a)**

5 a. **Rhea Silvia**　b. **shepherd**　c. **Romulus**

6 a. **Mars**　b. **Tiber River**　c. **raised**　d. **argument**　e. **Rome**

- **Vocabulary Builder**

1 **priestess** 女祭司　　　　2 **overthrow** 推翻

3 **float** 漂浮；漂流　　　　4 **rescue** 援救；營救

11 Europe in the Middle Ages 中世紀的歐洲

羅馬帝國於西元 476 年滅亡，羅馬人一度掌控了地中海沿岸所有地區和大部分的歐洲。到了西元 300 和 400 年代時，羅馬帝國已壯大到無法單靠一人管理，因此分裂為二：西羅馬帝國和東羅馬帝國。

西羅馬帝國在西元 476 年被入侵的日耳曼蠻族佔領。而東羅馬帝國，又稱為拜占庭帝國，則一直延續到西元 1453 年。自西羅馬帝國衰亡後到西元 1400 年代的這段時期，我們稱之為「中世紀」。

由於多數歐洲人都是文盲，中世紀早期常被稱作「黑暗時期」。對大部分歐洲人而言，這段時期的日子非常艱危，許多人死於戰爭、飢荒和疾病。

然而，對於基督教會來說，中世紀卻是成長的時期。西元 313 年，基督教在君士坦丁大帝的任命下，正式成為羅馬帝國法定宗教，並且持續擴張甚至延續到西羅馬帝國滅亡之後。到了西元 800 年，查理曼大帝統一大部分的西歐，其大軍所到之處，基督教也隨之傳開。最終，基督教會逐漸變得富裕而強盛。

- **Main Idea and Details**

1 **(a)**　　2 **(c)**　　3 **(b)**　　4 **(c)**　　5 **(b)**

6 a. **western**　b. **Germanic**　c. **hunger**
　 d. **Emperor Constantine**

- **Vocabulary Builder**

1 **split** 分裂　　　　　　2 **invader** 侵略者；入侵者

3 **expand** 擴張；發展　　4 **troops** 軍隊

12 Feudalism 封建制度

中世紀期間興起了一種獨特的社會制度，稱為封建制度，主要盛行於英格蘭、法國和德國。

在封建制度下，土地被用來交換服務。在許多地方，國王會將他們的土地分成封地。封地是由地方領主所掌控的大片土地，而領主會再將封地分給他的附庸們。附庸收到屬於自己的小封地，唯有效忠他們的國王或領主，才能繼續持有他們的封地。附庸、領主和國王都必須宣誓遵守這些條約。

附庸為領主或國王效勞的一種方式，就是在他們有需要的時候派出騎士。騎士宣誓對領主和國王效忠。在戰爭中，騎士們身著金屬盔甲，通常騎馬作戰。

封建社會的最底層是被稱為農奴或僱農的小農夫。農奴沒有太多權力，他們必須在領主的莊園上工作，沒有領主的允許不能離開莊園。

- **Main Idea and Details**

1 **(b)**　　2 **(c)**　　3 **(b)**　　4 **(a)**

5 a. **fief**　b. **oaths**　c. **Serfs/Peasants**

6 a. **lords**　b. **vassals**　c. **knights**　d. **manors**

- **Vocabulary Builder**

1 **feudalism** 封建制度　　2 **swear** 宣誓

3 **serf/peasant** 農奴；僱農　4 **manor** 莊園

Vocabulary Review 3

A

1 **Italian**　　　　　2 **republic**

3 **consuls**　　　　4 **Carthage**

5 **founded**　　　　6 **thrown**

7 **grew up**　　　　8 **Tiber River**

B

1 **Western**　　　　2 **Dark Ages**

3 **Christianity**　　4 **wealthy**

5 **feudalism**　　　6 **Fiefs**

7 **loyalty**　　　　8 **peasants**

C

1 **peninsula** 半島　　　2 **the Senate** 元老院

3 **expand** 擴張；發展　4 **shepherd** 牧羊人

5 **knight** 騎士　　　　6 **vassal** 附庸；封臣

D

1 貴族 **d**　　　　　　2 驅逐 **b**

3 推翻 **h**　　　　　　4 爭吵 **c**

5 分裂 **a**　　　　　　6 侵略者 **g**

7 法定的；正式的 **j**　8 封建制度 **f**

9 宣誓 **e**　　　　　　10 盔甲 **i**

Wrap-Up Test 1

A

1 **borders**　　　　2 **empty**

3 **imported**　　　4 **Merchants**

5 **Egyptians**　　　6 **preserve**

7 **brilliant**　　　8 **thinkers**

9 **service**　　　　10 **Middle Ages**

B

1 山脈　　　　　　2 路線

3 定位圖　　　　　4 貨船

5 商人　　　　　　6 香料

7 地形　　　　　　8 邊界

9 陡峭的　　　　　10 支流

11 乾燥的　　　　　12 關稅

13 干涉　　　　　　14 象形文字

15 木乃伊　　　　　16 紀念碑

17 混亂	18 保存
19 輝煌的	20 反叛
21 半島	22 元老院
23 女祭司	24 牧羊人
25 騎士	26 貴族
27 推翻	28 附庸；封臣
29 封地；采邑	30 封建制度

13 What Is the Scientific Method? 何謂科學方法？

當你對周遭的事物感到好奇時，你偶爾會問「為什麼」嗎？科學家們也常對世上的事物提出疑問，當他們想找出問題的答案時，會用一種稱為「科學方法」的詰問技巧。「科學方法」是科學家用來解決問題、探究事物運作原理的方法。

科學家通常使用下列五步驟的科學方法：

❶ 觀察並提出問題

科學家們仔細地觀察事物並提出問題。針對問題進行問答是詰問的基礎。

❷ 提出假設

科學家根據他們的觀察做出假設，一個成功的假設必須能夠透過實驗來檢驗。

❸ 進行實驗

第三個步驟是進行實驗，實驗對驗證假設非常重要。

❹ 蒐集並分析資料

資料的蒐集與分析是實驗過程的重要部分。通常科學家會運用數學技巧來蒐集和分析資料。

❺ 做出結論

最後，該是做結論的時刻了。實驗結果是否支持這個假設？如果這個假設不正確，科學家必須提出另一個假設並再次驗證。

- **Main Idea and Details**
1 **(a)**　　2 **(c)**　　3 **(c)**　　4 **(b)**
5 a. **inquiry**　　b. **hypothesis**　　c. **conclusion**
6 a. **inquiry** b. **hypothesis** c. **experiments** d. **data**
　e. **Draw**
- **Vocabulary Builder**
1 **observation** 觀察
2 **hypothesis** 假設
3 **interpret** 解釋；理解
4 **draw a conclusion** 下結論

14 Scientific Tools 科學工具

科學家們在實驗室裡進行許多工作。這些實驗室裡經常充滿了各種不同的科學工具和儀器，科學家使用工具來測量、觀察和操作物品。

科學家會使用量杯、燒杯或量筒，來測量液體的體積。溫度計用來測量溫度；磅秤測量重量；直尺衡量長度。

有時科學家需要仔細地觀察一樣物品。當他們想要觀察物品的細節時，可能會使用手持式放大鏡或者放大鏡。這些小型的手持式工具有將物體放大的功能。對於極小的物體，科學家可能會使用顯微鏡，將物體放大好幾倍來觀察。

科學家用鑷子夾取微小的物體。需要加熱物品時，可能會使用本生燈。

最後，實驗室裡首重安全性。因此，科學家通常會穿實驗衣，配戴護目鏡和手套來保護身體，這些也是重要的工具。

- **Main Idea and Details**
1 **(c)**　　2 **(c)**　　3 **(a)**　　4 **(b)**　　5 **(a)**
6 a. **beaker**　　b. **thermometer**　　c. **magnifying glass**
　d. **forceps**　　e. **gloves**
- **Vocabulary Builder**
1 **laboratory/lab** 實驗室
2 **manipulate** 操作
3 **beaker** 燒杯
4 **forceps** 鑷子

15 What Are Cells? 何謂細胞？

細胞是構成生命的基本單位，所有生物都由細胞組成。有機體不論體型大小，至少都由一個或一個以上的細胞組成。

植物和動物細胞有許多相同的部分。所有的細胞都有細胞核，是細胞的控制中心。包覆細胞的外層是細胞膜。植物和動物細胞都充滿細胞質。

但是植物細胞有幾個不同之處。植物細胞有細胞壁，是細胞膜外側的硬層。植物另一個很重要的成分是葉綠體，葉綠體含有葉綠素，讓植物呈現綠色，並讓植物進行光合作用。

許多動物細胞有特殊的功用。舉例來說，有些細胞組合在一起構成了肌肉等身體組織。它們也能構成器官，如心臟、肝臟、肺臟和腎臟，這些器官在動物的身體裡都扮演重要的角色。

- **Main Idea and Details**
1 **(b)**　　2 **(b)**　　3 **(c)**　　4 **(a)**
5 a. **All plant and animal cells have a nucleus, a cell membrane, and cytoplasm.**
　b. **Plant cells have cell walls and chloroplasts.**
　c. **They can form tissues and create organs.**
6 a. **Cell membrane**　b. **chlorophyll**　c. **tissues**　d. **organs**
- **Vocabulary Builder**
1 **cell membrane** 細胞膜
2 **nucleus** 細胞核
3 **chloroplast** 葉綠體
4 **cytoplasm** 細胞質

16 Classifying Living Things 生物的分類

地球上有數百萬種動植物，所有生物的基本單位都是細胞。有些生物由單一細胞構成，其他如人類等則由數十億個不同的細胞所組成。

生物由其共同特徵來分門別類，其中一種分類方式是看細胞，科學家通常將單細胞生物跟多細胞生物互相對照。

地球上最小的生物是微生物，或稱顯微生物。它們的體積小到必須用顯微鏡才能看見。許多微生物都是單細胞生物。細菌、病毒和原生生物是三種不同的微生物，它們賴以為生的一切物質都包含於單一細胞中。

多數生物擁有不只一個細胞，我們稱之為多細胞生物。爬蟲類、魚類、兩棲類、哺乳類和鳥類都是多細胞生物，真菌和植物也是多細胞生物。

- **Main Idea and Details**

1 **(a)**　　2 **(c)**　　3 **(c)**　　4 **(b)**

5 a. **cell**　　b. **Microorganisms**　　c. **Multi-celled**

6 a. **microorganisms**　b. **viruses**　c. **reptiles**　d. **fungi**

- **Vocabulary Builder**

1 **microscopic** 微小的；用顯微鏡才能看見的

2 **bacteria** 細菌　　　　　　　3 **fungus** 真菌

4 **multi-celled** 多細胞的

Vocabulary Review 4

A

1 **scientific method**　　　　2 **inquiry**

3 **hypothesis**　　　　　　　4 **interpreting**

5 **manipulate**　　　　　　　6 **magnifies**

7 **forceps**　　　　　　　　　8 **laboratory**

B

1 **organism**　　　　　　　　2 **nucleus**

3 **cell walls**　　　　　　　　4 **photosynthesis**

5 **tissues**　　　　　　　　　6 **features**

7 **multi-celled**　　　　　　　8 **protists**

C

1 **draw a conclusion** 下結論　　2 **microscope** 顯微鏡

3 **cell** 細胞　　　　　　　　　4 **microorganism** 微生物

5 **chloroplast** 葉綠體　　　　　6 **magnify** 放大

D

1 詢問；質詢 **h**　　　　　　　2 假設 **i**

3 想出（答案等）**e**　　　　　4 下結論 **a**

5 操作 **j**　　　　　　　　　　6 細胞核 **d**

7 專門的 **f**　　　　　　　　　8 微生物 **g**

9 單細胞的 **b**　　　　　　　　10 多細胞的 **c**

17 What Is Heredity? 何謂遺傳？

你可曾想過自己為什麼會長得像父母？你也許有著和父親相同的眼睛顏色，或是和母親相似的鼻子，這些相似點其實都來自於「遺傳」。所謂「遺傳」就是雙親將一些特徵傳給子女。

遺傳的基本單位是基因，基因攜帶了生物要如何生長發展的指示。每個人的基因數量相同，但是基因指示卻不同，這也是每個人具有不同特徵的原因。

當精子和卵子結合時，基因就由雙親傳至後代。這代表著遺傳物質一半來自母親，一半來自父親，因此孩子會遺傳到雙親的特徵。

然而，基因有兩種類型，分別是顯性基因和隱性基因，顯性基因比隱性基因強大。隱性基因存在於體內，但不具任何作用。一個生物的特徵和外貌實際上由顯性基因決定。

- **Main Idea and Details**

1 **(c)**　　2 **(c)**　　3 **(a)**　　4 **(b)**　　5 **(b)**

6 a. **instructions**　b. **egg cell**　c. **traits**　d. **Recessive**

- **Vocabulary Builder**

1 **heredity** 遺傳　　　　　　2 **gene** 基因

3 **offspring** 後代；子女　　　4 **similarity** 相似點

18 What Are Traits? 何謂特徵？

特徵是生物獨有的特質，所有的生物都有不同的特徵。有些特徵只受基因影響，但有些特徵則是先天基因和後天教養結合的產物。我們可以將特徵分為兩類：遺傳特徵和習得特徵。

遺傳特徵來自於雙親。對於人類來說，眼睛的顏色、髮色和鼻子的形狀都是遺傳特徵。大象的體型和豹的斑點也是遺傳特徵。遺傳特徵只由上一代所遺傳的基因而決定，生物無法自行改變。

然而，習得特徵卻不同。後天的教養和環境能夠影響許多特徵。你無法改變你的眼睛顏色，但你可以藉由生活方式改變某些特徵。舉例來說，身高可以改變，如果你擁有健康飲食和運動，就能夠長得比基因訊息的設定還要高。懂得如何閱讀和騎腳踏車也是習得特徵。

- **Main Idea and Details**

1 **(b)**　　2 **(b)**　　3 **(c)**　　4 **(c)**

5 a. **A trait is a particular characteristic that organisms have.**

　　b. **Eye color, hair color, and the shape of the nose are all inherited traits that humans have.**

　　c. **Inherited traits come from one's parents.**

6 a. **parents**　b. **genes**　c. **environment**　d. **height**

- **Vocabulary Builder**

1 **trait** 特徵　　　　　　　　2 **inherited trait** 遺傳特徵

3 **learned trait** 習得特徵　　　4 **nurture** 養育；教養

19 The Formation of the Earth 地球的形成

地球形成於距今約四十五億年以前。在這段期間，地球歷經許多變化。科學家將地球的歷史分為數個不同的時期，稱為「地質年代表」。地質年代表分為好幾個年代，每個年代都是一段極長的時間。

最早的是前寒武紀，涵蓋了百分之九十的地球歷史，從地球創始一直到六億年以前都屬於前寒武紀。在這段期間，地球才剛開始形成，因此極度地炎熱。同時，大氣開始獲得氧氣，動植物開始生長。

接著是古生代，持續了約莫三億年。在此期間，地球的氧氣值已穩定，無脊椎動物、魚類和爬蟲類在此期間演化。

中生代持續了大約一億五千萬年，這個年代通常被視為恐龍的時代。恐龍主宰這個時期，但是小型哺乳動物也開始演化。

如今，我們生存在新生代，此年代已經延續了約六千五百萬年。科學家通常將此年代稱為哺乳動物的時代。

- **Main Idea and Details**

1 **(c)**　　2 **(c)**　　3 **(a)**　　4 **(b)**

5 a. **oxygen**　b. **Paleozoic Era**　c. **Mesozoic Era**

6 a. **oxygen**　b. **reptiles**　c. **dinosaurs**　d. **current**

- Vocabulary Builder
1 **geologic time scale** 地質年代表
2 **Precambrian Era** 前寒武紀
3 **evolve** 進化；演化　　　4 **dominate** 主宰

20 Continental Drift 大陸漂移

今日的地球有七大陸塊，但地球的表面並非向來如此。科學家相信數百萬年以前，整個地球只有一塊叫做「盤古大陸」的超大陸。同時他們認為在地球的歷史上，這些陸塊曾經聚合後又數度分開。

這是怎麼發生的呢？「大陸漂移說」解釋了這個謎團，此學說表示地球的陸塊會緩慢地由一處移動到另一處。

所有的大陸都位於地殼上，地殼是由許多大型的板塊組成。地殼是固體，但是地殼底下的地函卻多為熾熱的熔岩，可如液體般流動。這些熔岩會帶動上面的地殼，因此板塊會持續不斷地移動。即便到了今日，這些陸塊每年都會移動數公釐。

於是造成地表不斷在變化。如果這些變化持續下去，再過百萬年後，地表將會變得截然不同。

- Main Idea and Details
1 **(a)**　　2 **(b)**　　3 **(b)**　　4 **(c)**　　5. **(b)**
6 a. **supercontinent**　b. **Pulled**　c. **crust**　d. **melted rock**
- Vocabulary Builder
1 **supercontinent** 超大陸　　2 **continental drift** 大陸漂移
3 **crust** 地殼　　　　　　　　4 **mantle** 地函

Vocabulary Review 5

A
1 **passing down**　　　　　2 **Genes**
3 **Dominant**　　　　　　　4 **Recessive**
5 **characteristic**　　　　　6 **Inherited**
7 **influence**　　　　　　　8 **information**
B
1 **time periods**　　　　　　2 **Precambrian**
3 **Paleozoic**　　　　　　　4 **dinosaurs**
5 **supercontinent**　　　　　6 **continental drift**
7 **melted rock**　　　　　　8 **continually**
C
1 **offspring** 後代；子女　　2 **gene** 基因
3 **trait** 特徵　　　　　　　4 **supercontinent** 超大陸
5 **plate** 板塊　　　　　　　6 **evolve** 進化；演化
D
1 遺傳 **f**　　　　　　　　2 特徵 **e**
3 影響 **a**　　　　　　　　4 結合 **c**
5 養育；教養 **d**　　　　　6 地質學的 **b**
7 穩定 **j**　　　　　　　　8 進化；演化 **i**
9 主宰 **g**　　　　　　　　10 學說；理論 **h**

21 Light and Heat 光和熱

光是一種以波傳遞的能量形式。光波每秒移動三十萬公里，所以比宇宙中的所有物體都快。地球上的主要光源是太陽。

光可以被反射和折射。光以直線前進直到撞擊某一物體為止。當光撞擊到物體，會自物體表面彈回。你可以從鏡中看見自己的影像，是光被鏡子反彈的緣故，這就是「反射」。而當光穿過一個物體，例如水，光線會彎曲，這就是「折射」。

熱是另一種能量形式。熱經由傳導、對流和輻射來傳遞。傳導是熱能藉由物體來傳遞。有些物質的導熱性非常好，例如金屬。對流是熱能在受熱液體或氣體中的傳遞，烤箱就是利用對流來運作。最後是輻射，它是不需要物質媒介的熱傳遞，太陽就是經由輻射來散發熱能。

- Main Idea and Details
1 **(b)**　　2 **(c)**　　3 **(a)**　　4 **(c)**
5 a. **They move 300,000 kilometers every second.**
　b. **Heat can be transferred by conduction, convection, and radiation.**
　c. **Conduction is the movement of heat by matter to carry it.**
6 a. **second**　b. **Refracted**　c. **matter**　d. **transfer**
- Vocabulary Builder
1 **reflection** 反射　　　　　2 **refraction** 折射
3 **conduction** 傳導　　　　　4 **convention** 對流

22 Electricity 電

電是一種能量形式，又分為靜電和電流。

靜電是藉由摩擦而在物體上產生的電荷，很短暫也有點難以預測。電流是穩定的電荷流，因為比較容易控制，所以比靜電更加實用。電流經由電線來傳導。

讓我們用電路來點亮一個燈泡。電路是電流通過的路徑，電流沿著電池和燈泡之間的路徑流動。當連接電池的線路封閉時，燈泡才會亮，由電池提供能量給電路，我們稱此為「閉路」。而「斷路」則使電流無法流通。

串聯電路只有一條路徑讓電流通過；並聯電路有兩條以上的電路讓電流通過。

- Main Idea and Details
1 **(a)**　　2 **(c)**　　3 **(b)**　　4 **(a)**
5 a. **static**　　b. **circuit**　　c. **open**
6 a. **unpredictable**　b. **steady**　c. **Parallel**　d. **Closed**
- Vocabulary Builder
1 **static electricity** 靜電　　　2 **current electricity** 電流
3 **closed circuit** 閉合電路；閉路　4 **parallel circuit** 並聯電路

23 Motion and Force 運動與力

宇宙中的每樣物體都會移動，舉凡太陽、地球、行星甚至所有星體，都在持續運動。

所有運動中的物體都有速度，也就是一個移動物體的速率。物體的位置是它所處的地點，而移動中的物體會不斷改變位置。

根據艾塞克‧牛頓爵士所發現的運動定律，運動中的物體會以同速度朝同方向持續移動，直到遭遇外力為止，這就是著名的「慣性定律」。

其中一種外力是地心引力。地心引力是地球與其他物體之間的吸引力，會將物體拉向地球。而萬有引力是作用於兩個物體之間，使之彼此吸引的力量。它能幫助地球繞著太陽運行，其他行星也藉由萬有引力運行在各自的軌道上。

摩擦力是另一種力，可以使移動中的物體減速或停止。當兩個物體互相摩擦，就會產生摩擦力。

• **Main Idea and Details**

1 **(a)**　　2 **(b)**　　3 **(b)**　　4 **(c)**　　5 **(c)**

6 a. **speed**　b. **motion**　c. **attraction**　d. **rub**

• **Vocabulary Builder**

1 **velocity** 速度　　　　2 **in motion** 運動中；移動中

3 **law of inertia** 慣性定律　　4 **friction** 摩擦力

24 Simple Machines 簡單機械

我們生活在一個機械的時代。機械是能工作的裝置，許多現代機械非常複雜，但大部分是以簡單機械為原理。簡單機械沒有太多構造，卻能讓人輕易地移動物品。一共有六種簡單機械。

斜面是一種傾斜的坡道，能使爬上爬下更輕鬆。

楔子是兩個斜面背靠背擺放而成，能夠固定、抬升或分開物體。門擋就是楔子的一種。

螺旋用來將兩個物體固定在一起，防止它們分開。

槓桿是一種簡易的桿子。我們在槓桿的另一端施力，就可用來移動物品。剪刀和鉗子都屬於槓桿。

滑輪是周圍有溝槽可纏繞繩索的的輪子。滑輪對於抬升重物非常有用，例如起重機。

輪軸屬於槓桿的一種，上面有「輪」連接到稱為「軸」的柱狀物。輪軸能夠改變轉力的大小，使施力更加輕鬆。球形門把和螺絲起子即是運用了輪軸的例子。

• **Main Idea and Details**

1 **(c)**　　2 **(a)**　　3 **(b)**　　4 **(c)**

5 a. **inclined plane**　b. **screw**　c. **wheel and axle**

6 a. **ramp**　b. **inclined**　c. **hold**　d. **grooved**　e. **axle**

• **Vocabulary Builder**

1 **lever** 槓桿　　　　2 **wheel and axle** 輪軸

3 **pulley** 滑輪　　　　4 **wedge** 楔子

Vocabulary Review 6

A

1 waves　　　　　　2 reflected
3 Refraction　　　　4 convection
5 rubbing　　　　　6 static
7 current　　　　　8 battery

B

1 velocity　　　　　2 force
3 Gravity　　　　　4 Gravitation
5 devices　　　　　6 inclined plane
7 lever　　　　　　8 grooved

C

1 refraction 折射　　　2 radiation 輻射
3 series circuit 串聯電路　4 gravity 地心引力
5 pulley 滑輪　　　　6 wedge 楔子

D

1 反射 **i**　　　　　2 傳導 **a**
3 輻射 **g**　　　　　4 短暫的 **b**
5 電路 **d**　　　　　6 速度 **c**
7 萬有引力 **h**　　　　8 摩擦力 **f**
9 裝置 **j**　　　　　10 複雜的 **e**

Wrap-Up Test 2

A

1 method　　　　　2 handheld
3 cytoplasm　　　　4 Inherited
5 comprised　　　　6 recessive
7 attraction　　　　8 Nurturing
9 bounces　　　　　10 charge

B

1 詢問；質詢　　　　2 假設
3 操作　　　　　　4 微小的；用顯微鏡才能看見的
5 葉綠體　　　　　6 放大
7 細胞核　　　　　8 微生物
9 細胞膜　　　　　10 多細胞的
11 後代；子女　　　　12 基因
13 精細胞　　　　　14 超大陸
15 板塊　　　　　　16 大陸漂移
17 遺傳　　　　　　18 特徵
19 養育；教養　　　　20 顯性的
21 隱性的　　　　　22 地質學的
23 使穩定　　　　　24 進化；演化
25 主宰　　　　　　26 學說；理論
27 反射　　　　　　28 輻射
29 速度　　　　　　30 萬有引力

25 Understanding Fractions
分數的進階觀念

分數是用來標示整體的一部分的數字。

上圖中，整體的每一等分是 $\frac{1}{4}$，我們把 $\frac{1}{4}$ 這種分數稱為「單位分數」。單位分數的分子是 1 。

當一個分數的分子大於或等於分母時，我們稱之為「假分數」。$\frac{5}{5}$、$\frac{4}{3}$ 和 $\frac{7}{6}$ 都是假分數。假分數可以寫成整數或是帶分數。分數線等同於除號，因此，分數 $\frac{5}{5}$ 等於5÷5 。而 5÷5 = 1，因此分數 $\frac{5}{5}$ 等於整數 1 。而 $\frac{4}{3}$ = 4÷3，因此 $\frac{4}{3}$ 也可以寫成帶分數 $1\frac{1}{3}$。

有些分數代表的量是相同的，例如 $\frac{1}{2}$ 和 $\frac{3}{6}$。$\frac{1}{2}$ = $\frac{3}{6}$，這種分數叫做「等值分數」。你把分子和分母乘上或除以相同的數字，就可以造出等值分數。

$$\frac{1}{2} = \frac{1\times3}{2\times3} = \frac{3}{6} \qquad \frac{3}{6} = \frac{3\div3}{6\div3} = \frac{1}{2} \qquad \frac{1}{2} = \frac{3}{6}$$

當分子和分母都沒有大於 1 的公因數時，此分數就是「最簡分數」。公因數是可同時除盡分子和分母的數字。舉例來說，$\frac{4}{8} = \frac{4\div4}{8\div4} = \frac{1}{2}$，由此可知，4 是 4 和 8 的公因數，$\frac{4}{8}$ 的最簡分數是 $\frac{1}{2}$。

可同時將分子和分母除盡的最大數字叫做最大公因數。舉例來說，$\frac{12}{16}$ 可以被2和4除盡。

$$\frac{12}{16} = \frac{12\div2}{16\div2} = \frac{6}{8} \qquad 或是 \qquad \frac{12}{16} = \frac{12\div4}{16\div4} = \frac{3}{4}$$

2 和 4 是 12 和 16 的公因數，4 則是 12 和 16 的最大公因數。

- **Main Idea and Details**

1 **(c)**　　2 **(c)**　　3 **(b)**　　4 **(b)**

5 a. **improper**　　b. **bar**　　c. **equivalent**

6 a. **greater**　b. **amount**　c. **denominator**　d. **4**

- **Vocabulary Builder**

1 **improper fraction** 假分數　　2 **unit fraction** 單位分數

3 **mixed number** 帶分數　　4 **simplest form** 最簡分數

26 Word Problems With Fractions 分數應用題

❶ $\frac{16}{20}$ 的公因數和最大公因數為何？

解答：$\frac{16\div2}{20\div2} = \frac{8}{10}$。$\frac{16\div4}{20\div4} = \frac{4}{5}$。

因為 $\frac{16}{20}$ 可被 2 和 4 除盡，2 和 4 就是 16 和 20 的公因數，4 是 $\frac{16}{20}$ 的最大公因數。

❷ 將 $\frac{12}{18}$ 化為最簡分數。

解答 1：將分子和分母同除以 2 。

$$\frac{12}{18} = \frac{12\div2}{18\div2} = \frac{6}{9}$$

因為 $\frac{6}{9}$ 還不是最簡分數，你可以再進一步同除以 3 。

$\frac{6\div3}{9\div3} = \frac{2}{3}$。由於 2 和 3 已經沒有大於 1 的公因數了，因此 $\frac{12}{18}$ 的最簡分數就是 $\frac{2}{3}$。

解答 2: 將分子和分母同除以最大公因數，就可以直接找出最簡分數。$\frac{12\div6}{18\div6} = \frac{2}{3}$。所以 $\frac{12}{18}$ 的最簡分數是 $\frac{2}{3}$。

❸ 比較分數 $\frac{2}{5}$ 和 $\frac{4}{5}$ 的大小。

解答：$\frac{2}{5} < \frac{4}{5}$。$\frac{4}{5}$ 大於 $\frac{2}{5}$。

當比較同分母的分數時，只要比較分子的大小。

❹ 比較分數 $\frac{2}{3}$ 和 $\frac{3}{6}$ 的大小。

解答：$\frac{2}{3} = \frac{2\times2}{3\times2} = \frac{4}{6}$。$\frac{4}{6} > \frac{3}{6}$。

因此 $\frac{2}{3}$ 大於 $\frac{3}{6}$。要比較異分母分數，必須先通分。所以要先找出 $\frac{2}{3}$ 的等值分數，且分母必須為 6 。一旦分母相同，你就可以輕易地比較它們。

- **Main Idea and Details**

1 **(a)**　　2 **(b)**　　3 **(b)**　　4 **(a)**　　5 **(c)**

6 a. **numerators**　　b. **greatest common factor**

　 c. **denominators**

- **Vocabulary Builder**

1 **solution** 解答　　　　　　　2 **reduce** 約分

3 **common denominator** 公分母

4 **unlike fractions** 異分母分數

27 Lines and Angles 線條和角度

當兩條直線、線段或是射線在同一點相交時，會形成一個角，而它們相交的點就叫做「頂點」。下圖是角 ABC。

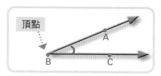

B 點是角 ABC 的頂點。也可以這樣寫：∠ ABC 或是 ∠ CBA。當替角命名時，一定要把頂點放在中間。

角的大小是以度（°）來測量。測量角度時，我們會使用一種測量工具叫做量角器。一個角量出來會介於 0 到 180 度之間。

角有四種，直角剛好 90°，兩條垂直線相交時就會形成直角。銳角比直角小，量出來大於 0° 並小於 90°。鈍角比直角大，量出來大於 90° 而小於 180°。平角是 180°，正好形成一直線。

- **Main Idea and Details**

1 **(b)**　　2 **(b)**　　3 **(c)**　　4 **(c)**

5 a. **A protractor can measure an angle.**

　 b. **An acute angle measures greater than 0° and less than 90°.**

　 c. **An obtuse angle measures greater than 90° and less than 180°.**

6 a. **vertex**　b. **degrees**　c. **Acute angle**　d. **180°**

- **Vocabulary Builder**

1 **vertex** 頂點　　　　　　　2 **protractor** 量角器

3 **perpendicular lines** 垂直線　4 **obtuse angle** 鈍角

28 Polygons, Triangles, and Circles 多邊形、三角形和圓形

多邊形是由三個以上的邊組成的封閉圖形。有四個邊的多邊形可以是正方形、矩形、平行四邊形、菱形或梯形。五個邊的多邊形是五邊形，六個邊的叫六邊形。

有三個邊的多邊形是三角形。三角形有許多種類，三個邊等長的三角形叫等邊三角形。兩個邊等長的三角形叫做等腰三角形。三個邊都不等長的三角形叫不等邊三角形。

此外，銳角三角形的所有內角均為銳角。直角三角形包含一個直角。鈍角三角形有一個內角是鈍角。

圓是封閉的圓形，圓上的每一點到圓心的距離都相等。圓有不同的結構，連接圓上任意兩點的線段叫做弦。直徑是把圓對分的弦，半徑是一端在圓心、一端在圓上的線段，半徑的長度是直徑的一半。

- **Main Idea and Details**

1 **(a)**　2 **(b)**　3 **(a)**　4 **(c)**

5 a. **polygon**　b. **equilateral**　c. **radius**

6 a. **rhombuses**　b. **scalene**　c. **obtuse**　d. **Chord**

- **Vocabulary Builder**

1 **parallelogram** 平行四邊形

2 **equilateral triangle** 等邊三角形

3 **chord** 弦　　　　　4 **radius** 半徑

Vocabulary Review 7

A

1 **numerator**	2 **division sign**
3 **equivalent**	4 **divided**
5 **common factors**	6 **simplest**
7 **denominators**	8 **unlike**

B

1 **angle**	2 **perpendicular**
3 **acute angle**	4 **right angle**
5 **polygon**	6 **equilateral**
7 **chord**	8 **bisects**

C

1 **improper fraction** 假分數	2 **reduce** 約分
3 **acute angle** 銳角	4 **protractor** 量角器
5 **parallelogram** 平行四邊形	6 **diameter** 直徑

D

1 公因數 **j**	2 最簡分數 **c**
3 解答 **f**	4 約分 **g**
5 公分母 **b**	6 異分母分數 **e**
7 直角 **a**	8 鈍角 **i**
9 等腰三角形 **d**	10 直徑 **h**

29 Prefixes and Suffixes 字首和字尾

字首和字尾是加在單字前面或後面的字母群，它們通常會添加字義，創造出新單字。

字首位於一個字的開頭。英文有很多字首，有些字首代表「沒有」或「不」的意思，包括 im-、in-、un-、dis- 和 non-。舉例來說，impossible 意指「不可能」，independent 意指「不依賴」，unhappy 意指「不快樂」，dishonest 意指「不誠實」。以下是一些常見的字首及其意義：

pre-	= 在前	預習
fore-	= 在……之前；預先	預測、前景
mid-	= 中間	期中的
inter-	= 在……之間；在……之中	中間的、國際的
re-	= 再（次）	重複、重做
mis-	= 錯誤的；錯誤地	拼錯、錯誤

字尾位於一個字的末端。英文有許多字尾，其中兩個相當常見的是 -ed 和 -ing。-ed 構成動詞的過去式，-ing 構成動詞的進行式。以下是一些其他常見的字尾和它們的意義：

-er	= ……的人	老師、農夫
-en	= 用……製成的	金製的
-ful	= 充滿……的	精采的
-able	= 能夠	可洗的
-less	= 沒有	疏忽的、無痛的

認識常用的字首和字尾是非常實用的。有時你將一些艱澀的單字拆解成字首、字根和字尾，就能理解它們的意思。

- **Main Idea and Details**

1 **(c)**　2 **(a)**　3 **(c)**　4 **(c)**　5 **(a)**

6 a. **beginning**　b. **end**　c. **continuous**　d. **figure out**

- **Vocabulary Builder**

1 **prefix** 字首　　　　　2 **suffix** 字尾

3 **continuous form** 進行式　4 **root** 字根

30 Tenses 時態

英文裡，所有的句子都有一個動詞。動詞用來描述句中的動作，可以表達現在正在發生、過去曾發生和未來將要發生的動作，我們稱之為「時態」。時態顯示動作發生的時間，主要的動詞時態有三種：過去式、現在式和未來式。

過去式描述「已經發生的事件」。

　　我昨天遇到我朋友。

　　她十年前住在紐約市。

現在式描述「現在正在發生的事件」。我們除了使用現在式來陳述事實，也會用來表示重覆或是習慣的動作。

　　我住在緬因街。

　　我早上都六點起床。

　　地球繞太陽旋轉。

未來式描述「未來將會發生的事件」。

> 我明天會去上學。

> 泰勒先生下星期會去找一份新工作。

這些是三種基本的時態，每種時態又可細分為不同形式：進行式和完成式。我們可以使用過去、現在和未來進行式，也可以使用過去、現在和未來完成式。

- **Main Idea and Details**

1 **(c)**　　2 **(b)**　　3 **(c)**　　4 **(b)**

5 a. **A verb shows the action in the sentence.**
　b. **The three main tenses are the past tense, the present tense, and the future tense.**
　c. **The future tense describes things that will occur in the future.**

6 a. **happened**　b. **happening**　c. **state**　d. **future**

- **Vocabulary Builder**

1 **future tense** 未來式
2 **present tense** 現在式
3 **repeated** 重複的；反覆的
4 **habitual** 習慣的

31 Complete Sentences 英文完整句

句子是表達一個完整想法的一組單字。一個完整的句子包含一個主詞和一個述語，主詞說明該句子描述的對象，述語說明句中的主詞是什麼或做什麼。

主詞	述語
約翰	吃東西。
她	看電視。
我大哥	每天去上學。

主詞通常是名詞或代名詞，而且一般出現在句子的最前面。述語必須包含一個動詞，也可含有其他詞性的詞。

「句子片斷」是句子的一部分，或是一個不完整的句子，可能缺少主詞或動詞，並且無法表達完整的意思。

句子片斷	完整句子
去看電影	我去看電影。
上週末的電影	我上週末去看電影。

複合句包含兩個以上的完整句子，這些句子由逗號和連接詞連接，如 and、but、so 和 or。

> 我喜歡橘子，而我姊姊也喜歡橘子。

> 我們待在家裡，但是詹姆士出門了。

如果不使用逗號或連接詞連接兩個句子，就會變成連寫句。

連寫句	完整句子
小心別動。	小心，而且別動。
我說英文約翰說中文。	我說英文，而約翰說中文。
	我說英文。約翰說中文。

- **Main Idea and Details**

1 **(b)**　　2 **(a)**　　3 **(c)**　　4 **(c)**

5 a. **subject**　b. **fragment**　c. **compound**

6 a. **subject**　b. **incomplete**　c. **comma**　d. **conjunction**

- **Vocabulary Builder**

1 **predicate** 述語
2 **sentence fragment** 句子片斷；不完整句
3 **run-on sentence** 連寫句；不斷句
4 **compound sentence** 複合句

32 Proofreading 校對

閱讀下列段落，裡面共有 9 個錯誤，使用校對符號來訂正這些錯誤。

校對符號	
~~go~~ went	用線劃掉錯別字，並在上方寫上正確的字。
∧	插入字或標點符號。
ℒ	刪除錯字和標點符號。
≡	大寫
/	小寫

潔西卡每個週末都會做一些瘋狂事。上個星期六，她決定和她的朋友蒂娜去遊樂園玩。潔西卡和蒂娜一大早就坐公車抵達遊樂園，以避開中午以後的人潮，而且，也不用排隊排很久。

潔西卡愛玩雲霄飛車，蒂娜也是。她們玩了幾趟之後，接著也去玩碰碰車。她們開始覺得累了，於是買了一些零食和飲料，坐了一會兒。潔西卡想再多玩幾趟，但是蒂娜不想。遊樂園的人潮越來越多，所以每次要玩都得排隊排得更久。潔西卡和蒂娜決定回家。她們這一天玩得很高興，到了公車站牌後就坐車回家了。

- **Main Idea and Details**

1 **(a)**　　2 **(b)**　　3 **(a)**　　4 **(c)**　　5 **(b)**

6 a. **capitalize**　b. **delete**　c. **lowercase**

- **Vocabulary Builder**

1 **proofread** 校對
2 **capitalize** 用大寫書寫
3 **insert** 插入
4 **punctuation** 標點符號

Vocabulary Review 8

A

1 added
2 prefixes
3 breaking
4 action
5 takes place
6 describes
7 repeated
8 future

B

1 complete
2 predicate
3 verb
4 fragment
5 compound
6 conjunction
7 proofreading
8 incorrect

C

1 **suffix** 字尾　　　　　　　　2 **root** 字根

3 **sentence fragment** 句子片斷；不完整句

4 **conjunction** 連接詞　　　　5 **proofread** 校對

6 **habitual** 習慣的

D

1 字首 **h**　　　　　　　　　　2 分解 **a**

3 字根 **f**　　　　　　　　　　4 發生 **b**

5 描述 **i**　　　　　　　　　　6 習慣的 **e**

7 述語 **g**　　　　　　　　　　8 複合句 **j**

9 不正確的 **c**　　　　　　　　10 插入 **d**

33 The Art of the Middle Ages 中世紀的藝術

中世紀持續了大約一千年，直到十五世紀才結束。在這段期間，歐洲建造了許多雄偉的哥德式大教堂，大部分的藝術也受到基督教教會的影響。

許多哥德式大教堂有著高聳入雲的高塔和尖塔。教堂的巍峨和雄偉氣度，激起了人們的虔誠心。挑高的天花板、繪畫和彩繪玻璃窗，描述著《聖經》裡的故事，也營造出令人肅然起敬的空間。

哥德式大教堂的另一大特色是扶壁。由於這種教堂相當高聳而宏偉，因此運用了一種稱為「扶壁」的石造支柱，支撐著教堂避免崩塌。大教堂也常可見到稱為「滴水獸」的魔鬼石雕。法國的巴黎聖母院和夏特爾大教堂即是兩座聞名遐邇的中世紀大教堂。

最璀璨的一些中世紀藝術也可在一種稱為「泥金裝飾手抄本」的書籍中見到。在中世紀期間，書籍通常由僧侶們手抄而成。他們用金箔和銀箔來繪圖，以鮮明華麗的圖案裝飾書籍的許多內頁。《凱爾經》即是著名的泥金裝飾手抄本。

- **Main Idea and Details**

1 **(a)**　　　2 **(c)**　　　3 **(a)**　　　4 **(b)**

5 a. **Stone braces called buttresses supported Gothic cathedrals.**
　 b. **Tall ceilings, paintings, and stained-glass windows depicting stories from the Bible created awe-inspiring spaces.**
　 c. **People made books by hand in the Middle Ages.**

6 a. **ceilings**　b. **statues**　c. **Cathedral**　d. **by hand**
　 e. **illuminated**

- **Vocabulary Builder**

1 **gargoyle** 滴水獸

2 **awe-inspiring** 令人肅然起敬的

3 **buttress** 扶壁

4 **illuminated manuscript** 泥金裝飾手抄本

34 The Art of Islam and Africa 伊斯蘭教和非洲藝術

世界各地的藝術林林總總，形色各異。

在中世紀時期，來自北非的穆斯林征服了大半的西班牙，他們發展出一種迥異於哥德式的建築風格。

伊斯蘭建築的一個主要特色就是喚拜塔。大部分的清真寺──伊斯蘭教的朝拜場所──有四個喚拜塔，也就是座落於清真寺四個角落的高塔。許多伊斯蘭建築也會有圓頂，也就是建築物上面的圓形屋頂或天花板。位於以色列耶路撒冷的圓頂清真寺，和印度阿格拉的泰姬瑪哈陵，是兩座相當優美的伊斯蘭建築。

在非洲，藝術家會製作雕像和面具。很久以前，許多非洲人並不會以文字記錄他們的歷史，而是藉由歌唱、舞蹈和製作藝術品，來記憶過去的事件。為了紀念他們的祖先，他們會刻製雕像並製作許多面具。雕刻一般以赤陶土或黃銅製成，描繪著人物和動物形象。面具則呈現各種臉譜，非洲人會帶著它們表演面具舞。

- **Main Idea and Details**

1 **(b)**　　　2 **(c)**　　　3 **(a)**　　　4 **(a)**

5 a. **mosque**　　b. **Domes**　　c. **ancestors**

6 a. **tower**　　b. **roof**　　c. **masks**　　d. **sculptures**

- **Vocabulary Builder**

1 **mosque** 清真寺

2 **minaret** 喚拜塔；叫拜樓（清真寺的尖塔）

3 **brass** 黃銅

4 **terra cotta** 赤陶土

35 Musical Notation 樂譜

樂譜的發明，使得世界各地不同語言的人們都能看懂並且唱奏音樂。

詞曲創作人和作曲家用一種叫做「樂譜」的特殊書寫方式來寫下他們的音樂。只要你會看樂譜，不論樂曲有多複雜，你都可以隨意地演唱或彈奏出來。

讓我們來認識樂譜的一些結構吧。五線譜上面寫著音符，音符基本上可以告訴我們音樂的旋律、長度和音高。有時候，音符上面會有一個圓點，我們稱之為附點音符，用來告訴演奏者將音長延長一半。有時候，兩個音符之間會由一條弧線連結，叫做連結線，告訴演奏者將第一個音延續到第二個音而不間斷。

每首樂曲的開頭會有拍號，都由兩個數字組成，如 $\frac{4}{4}$、$\frac{3}{4}$、$\frac{2}{4}$。拍號代表這首樂曲的節拍或拍子，指示演奏者該如何演奏這首樂曲。

作曲家通常將音樂分為很多小節。單小節線用來表示小節的開始與結束，雙小節線則用來表示整首樂曲的結束。

- **Main Idea and Details**

1 **(a)**　　2 **(b)**　　3 **(a)**　　4 **(c)**　　5 **(c)**

6 a. **pitch**　b. **Tie**　c. **meter**　d. **Single bar line**

- **Vocabulary Builder**
1 **musical notation** 樂譜；音樂記譜法
2 **double bar line** 雙小節線
3 **tie** 連結線
4 **measure** 小節

36 Composers and Their Music
樂曲家和他們的音樂

古典音樂界有許多傑出的作曲家，其中三位是約翰‧塞巴斯蒂安‧巴哈、喬治‧弗里德里希‧韓德爾和約瑟夫‧海頓。

巴哈是巴洛克時期的德國作曲家和風琴家，他創作過無數音樂作品，包含管風琴曲、協奏曲、清唱套曲和大量的教堂合唱曲。《布蘭登堡協奏曲》和《馬太受難曲》是巴哈最廣為人知的幾部代表作。

韓德爾也是德國的巴洛克音樂作曲家，然而，韓德爾大多數的時間都住在英格蘭，並且使用英文創作歌詞。他最為人所知的就是作品皆取材於《聖經》故事，由管弦樂隊搭配合唱團所演出的著名《彌賽亞》即為其一。其中的《哈利路亞大合唱》是所有古典音樂中最廣為流傳的曲子之一。

海頓是古典時期繼巴哈和韓德爾之後的作曲家，或被譽為交響樂之父，創作過百餘首交響樂，《驚愕交響曲》和《創世紀》是他最著名的交響樂曲。他是最偉大的古典音樂作曲家之一路德維希‧范‧貝多芬的老師，人們也因此而紀念他。

- **Main Idea and Details**
1 (c)　　2 (a)　　3 (a)　　4 (c)
5 a. **Baroque**　　b. **Handel**　　c. **Haydn**
6 a. **Baroque**　　b. **lyrics**　　c. **Bible**　　d. **Classical**
　　e. **Symphony**

- **Vocabulary Builder**
1 **lyrics** 歌詞
2 **cantata** 清唱套曲；康塔塔
3 **symphony** 交響樂
4 **composition**（大型）樂曲

Vocabulary Review 9
A
1 **cathedrals**
2 **collapsing**
3 **medieval**
4 **copied**
5 **Muslims**
6 **minaret**
7 **statues**
8 **carved**
B
1 **Songwriters**
2 **notes**
3 **time signature**
4 **measures**
5 **outstanding**
6 **Baroque**
7 **Bible**
8 **symphonies**
C
1 **buttress** 扶壁
2 **demon** 惡魔
3 **minaret** 喚拜塔；叫拜樓（清真寺的尖塔）
4 **composition**（大型）樂曲
5 **dotted note** 附點音符
6 **time signature** 拍號

D
1 激勵；激起 h
2 令人肅然起敬的 c
3 樂譜；音樂記譜法 e
4 描寫 j
5 清真寺 f
6 小節 i
7 傑出的 d
8 為數眾多的 a
9 合唱音樂 b
10（大型）樂曲 g

Wrap-Up Test 3
A
1 **numerator**
2 **denominators**
3 **acute angle**
4 **diameter**
5 **Prefixes**
6 **compound**
7 **tense**
8 **incomplete**
9 **cathedrals**
10 **notation**
B
1 假分數
2 等值分數
3 射線
4 量角器
5 平行四邊形
6 半徑
7 公因數
8 最簡分數
9 公分母
10 異分母分數
11 鈍角
12 等腰三角形
13 直徑
14 字尾
15 句子片斷；不完整句
16 連接詞
17 校對符號
18 遊樂園
19 分解
20 發生
21 述語
22 複合句
23 插入
24 中世紀的
25 扶壁
26 喚拜塔；叫拜樓（清真寺的尖塔）
27 拍號
28 令人肅然起敬的
29 樂譜；音樂記譜法
30（大型）樂曲

FUN學 美國英語閱讀課本 6
各學科實用課文

Authors

Michael A. Putlack
Michael A. Putlack graduated from Tufts University in Medford, Massachusetts, USA, where he got his B.A. in History and English and his M.A. in History. He has written a number of books for children, teenagers, and adults.

e-Creative Contents
A creative group that develops English contents and products for ESL and EFL students.

作者	Michael A. Putlack & e-Creative Contents
翻譯	丁宥暄
編輯	丁宥榆／丁宥暄
校對	陳慧莉
製程管理	洪巧玲
發行人	黃朝萍
出版者	寂天文化事業股份有限公司
電話	+886-(0)2-2365-9739
傳真	+886-(0)2-2365-9835
網址	www.icosmos.com.tw
讀者服務	onlineservice@icosmos.com.tw
出版日期	2023 年 10 月 二版二刷（寂天雲隨身聽 APP 版）

國家圖書館出版品預行編目 (CIP) 資料

FUN 學美國英語閱讀課本：各學科實用課文（寂天雲隨身聽 APP 版） / Michael A. Putlack, e-Creative Contents 著；丁宥暄，鄭玉瑋譯 . -- 二版 . -- [臺北市] : 寂天文化，2023.10- 冊； 公分

ISBN 978-626-300-221-0 (第 6 冊：平裝)

1. 英語 2. 讀本

805.18

FUN學 6

美國英語閱讀課本
各學科實用課文 二版

AMERICAN SCHOOL TEXTBOOK

READING KEY

Workbook

作者 Michael A. Putlack & e-Creative Contents　譯者 丁宥暄

01 Reading Maps

Listen to the passage and fill in the blanks.

🎧 37

There are many different kinds of _____.

A _____ map shows where cities, states, and countries are located.

Political maps use lines to show _____ borders, such as state and

country _____.

A _____ map shows landforms and bodies of water. Landforms are

different _____ ____ land on the earth's surface. _____ ____ _____

include oceans, rivers, and lakes. These maps rely on colors to _____

different geographical features. For _____, water is blue, mountains are

brown, and forests are green. These maps are also called _____ maps.

A _____ map is a map that shows information about past _____

and where they occurred. Historical maps often have _____ in their titles.

A road map and a _____ map focus on roads and streets. They

show important buildings and transportation _____ such as airports,

railroads, and highways.

Sometimes, you can see a small map _____ _____ the main map. We call

it a "locator" or "_____ map." It shows where the area of the main map is

_____.

B Write the meaning of each word or phrase from Word List (main book p.104)
in English.

1	行政區域圖	_____	9	地理的	_____
2	領土的	_____	10	特徵	_____
3	邊界	_____	11	歷史地圖	_____
4	自然地圖	_____	12	道路地圖	_____
5	地形	_____	13	專注於	_____
6	水域	_____	14	路線	_____
7	依賴	_____	15	設置在……之上	_____
8	顯示	_____	16	定位圖；定位地圖	_____

02 Mountains, Rivers, and Deserts of the World

A Listen to the passage and fill in the blanks. 🎧38

Mountains are high landforms with _____ sides. They often form mountain _____ or mountain _____. The _____ Mountains are in Asia. Mt. Everest, the world's highest mountain, and many other _____ _____ are located there. In Europe, there are the _____. South America has the _____ Mountains. And North America has the _____ and the Rocky Mountains.

Rivers are long _____ of water that flow into another body of water. Their _____ —the starting place of a river—may be high in a mountain. Then, they _____ until they reach the sea. Many _____ also empty into large rivers. The longest river in the world is the _____ River in Africa. The Amazon River in South America is another _____ river. In the United States, the _____ River is called the "mighty Mississippi."

_____ are very dry land with few plants and animals. They get very little _____, so most deserts are both hot and _____. But they can be cold, too. _____ is an example of a cold desert. The world's biggest desert is the _____ in Africa. Next is the _____ Desert in the Middle East. The _____ Desert in Asia is another huge desert.

B Write the meaning of each word or phrase from Word List in English.

1	陡峭的	_____	7	支流	_____
2	側面；斜坡	_____	8	流入	_____
3	山脈	r _____	9	巨大的；浩瀚的	_____
4	山脈	c _____	10	降雨；降雨量	_____
5	山峰	_____	11	乾燥的	_____
6	源頭；水源	_____	12	南極洲	_____

03 A World of Trade

A 🗨 Listen to the passage and fill in the blanks. 🎧 39

We live in a _____ world. This means that every area on the _____ is in contact with every other area. One way that people _____ each other is through trade. Trade is the buying and selling of _____ and services.

Trade between different countries is called _____ trade. Many companies try to sell their goods all _____ the world. When they send their goods to another country, they are _____ them. Many companies buy _____ and other products from other countries as well. When they bring in goods from another country, they are _____ them. Most _____ try to export more than they import.

Many times, when goods are imported, the _____ must pay a tariff. A _____ is a tax that a government _____ on imported goods. Trade that has no taxes or government _____ is called free trade.

Many of the world's countries have free market _____. In a _____ _____ economy, people decide what to produce and what to buy. However, in some countries, the government _____ what is bought and sold.

B 🗨 Write the meaning of each word or phrase from Word List in English.

1	全球化	_____	7	購買者	_____
2	地球；行星	_____	8	關稅	_____
3	與……聯繫	_____	9	干涉	_____
4	國際貿易	_____	10	自由貿易	_____
5	出口	_____	11	自由市場經濟	_____
6	進口	_____	12	控制	_____

Daily Test 04 Ancient Trade

A Listen to the passage and fill in the blanks. 🎧 40

Why do people _____? People trade with each other because they both

_____. Countries around the world have different natural resources and

_____ resources. People in each country produce different goods

_____ these resources. They trade these _____ for goods they do not

produce. That is trade.

_____ _____ transportation and communication, people around the world

can trade more _____ today than ever before.

Long ago, people also traded with _____ _____. Thousands of years

ago, there were no _____ _____, airplanes, telephones, or computers.

But people still _____ international trade.

For instance, people in ancient Greece used to trade with others around the

_____ _____. Greeks made beautiful _____ and grew

olives and grapes. They traded these items for goods they _____. Greek

ships often _____ across the sea to Egypt. In Egypt, they _____

their products for cotton, fruit, and wheat.

The ancient _____ also traded for many goods with Egypt and other

nearby countries. The Romans also traded with China and _____.

_____ used a route called the Silk Road to go to China. They traded

gold and _____ _____ for silk, gems, and spices from China and India.

B Write the meaning of each word or phrase from Word List in English.

1 受益；受惠 _____
2 人力資源 _____
3 物品 _____
4 由於 _____
5 通訊 _____
6 貨船 _____

7 進行 _____
8 地中海 _____
9 陶器 _____
10 以……作為交換；拿……來以物易物 _____
11 商人 _____
12 香料 _____

A Listen to the passage and fill in the blanks. 🎧 41

One of the earliest human _____ formed in Egypt about _____

years ago. It was _____ on the Nile River. The land around the Nile was

very _____ because the river _____ every year. During the _____,

the river left rich topsoil and _____ on the land. This let farmers grow many

_____. Soon, Egypt had a large _____.

Ancient Egypt was ruled by _____. They were kings, but people

believed the pharaohs were _____ from gods. As god-kings, the

pharaohs ruled over the _____, who were slaves.

The ancient Egyptians were great _____ and builders. They built

enormous _____ that were tombs for the pharaohs. They also built the

_____ near the pyramids. And they constructed many other stone

temples and _____ throughout the land.

The ancient Egyptians developed a writing system called _____. It

used pictures and symbols that _____ ideas, sound, and objects.

Hieroglyphics were _____ on walls and monuments.

B Write the meaning of each word or phrase from Word List in English.

1 文明 _____
2 集中於 _____
3 肥沃的 _____
4 氾濫 _____
5 表土 _____
6 淤泥 _____
7 人口 _____
8 法老（古埃及國王）_____
9 是……的後裔 _____
10 建造 _____
11 （古希臘、羅馬、埃及的）神殿 _____
12 紀念碑 _____
13 象形文字 _____
14 被雕刻於…… _____

06 The Culture of Egypt

A Listen to the passage and fill in the blanks. 🎧42

The ancient Egyptians _____ many gods. They often had both
human and animal _____. The most important god was _____, the
sun god. He had a _____ head. The pharaoh was believed to be a _____
of Ra. Horus, another god of the sun, had the head of a _____. Anubis, the
god of the dead, had the head of a _____. Set, or Seth, was the god of
_____. Osiris _____ the underworld. Isis, the sister and wife of
_____ and the mother of Horus, was the goddess of
_____. She also protected people from _____ and harm.
The pharaohs were both _____ and powerful. Menes became the first
_____ of Egypt when he united two _____.
_____ _____ was the greatest and most powerful pharaoh of all. He
conquered many lands. Egypt was the most _____ during the reign
of Amenhotep III.
The ancient Egyptians believed they would have new _____ after they died.
So the culture of Egypt centered on life after _____. They developed a
way to preserve the _____ and could make a body a _____. Also,
Egyptian _____ contained everything a person would need in the next
life.

B Write the meaning of each word or phrase from Word List in English.

1 信奉 _____
2 外貌 _____
3 隼；獵鷹 _____
4 豺狼；胡狼 _____
5 混亂 _____
6 陰間 _____
7 生育力 _____

8 王國 _____
9 繁榮的 _____
10 統治時期 _____
11 保存 _____
12 死者 _____
13 木乃伊 _____

07 Ancient Greece

A Listen to the passage and fill in the blanks. 🎧 43

One of the most _____ of all ancient civilizations was found in Greece. The Greek people lived in many different _____. Most city-states were built around an _____, a walled hill where people could _____ safety from attack. The city-states often _____ against each other. But, when foreign _____ like the Persians attacked, they _____ and fought together.

_____ and Sparta were the two most powerful city-states in _____ Greece. They had different _____ and cultures.

Athens was the birthplace of _____. In Athens, citizens were allowed to vote and to _____ _____ in the government. But only _____ could be citizens. The Spartans were _____. They were great _____. Spartan boys were _____ to be soldiers from a young age. Even Spartan girls were trained to _____ in sporting events. Athens and Sparta fought the _____ War against each other. In the end, Sparta _____ Athens.

The Greeks produced many great artists, scientists, _____, politicians, and generals. However, in the fourth century _____, Alexander the Great _____ all of the Greek city-states and united them in his empire.

B Write the meaning of each word or phrase from Word List in English.

1 輝煌的　_____
2 （古希臘的）城邦　_____
3 （古希臘城市的）衛城　_____
4 有圍牆的；有城牆的　_____
5 尋求　_____
6 團結　_____
7 出生地；發源地　_____

8 參與……　_____
9 戰士　_____
10 訓練　_____
11 競賽　_____
12 伯羅奔尼撒戰爭　_____
13 擊敗　_____
14 將軍　_____

08 Socrates and Plato

A Listen to the passage and fill in the blanks. 🎧44

The ancient Greeks produced many great _____ and philosophers. Greek philosophers studied history, political science, and _____. They often _____ students as well. The two _____ of all were Socrates and Plato.

_____ was a teacher in Athens. He led _____ about ways to live. He used a form of _____ called the Socratic Method. Basically, he would ask _____ questions. These questions were _____ to find the answer to a problem. Or the questions would show the _____, such as Socrates, how little he actually knew. Socrates _____ many leading Athenians because he began to question the city's laws, customs, and _____. Socrates was put on _____ for "urging Athens' young people to _____." He was found _____ and sentenced to death.

Socrates _____ many students. One of them was named _____. Plato wrote down all of Socrates' _____. He _____ many different books. Most of them were _____ involving Socrates and other famous _____. One of the most _____ was the *The Republic*. It described the _____ of government in Plato's mind. Plato's _____ became very important and helped _____ all of Western philosophy.

B Write the meaning of each word or phrase from Word List in English.

1	思想家	_____	8	煽動	_____
2	政治學	_____	9	反叛	_____
3	一連串的；一系列的	_____	10	有罪的	_____
4	目的是……	_____	11	被處死刑	_____
5	發問者	_____	12	牽涉	_____
6	使惱怒	_____	13	理想的	_____
7	審判	_____	14	建立	_____

Listen to the passage and fill in the blanks. ∩45

Early in its history, Rome was a small city _____ on the Tiber River of the

Italian _____. As Rome grew, its army conquered many _____

countries. By _____ B.C., Rome had conquered most of the _____

peninsula.

For 250 years, Rome was _____ by Etruscan kings. In 510 B.C., the Romans

_____ the king and founded the Roman Republic. A _____

is a form of government in which the government's leaders are _____ by

the people.

Every year, the _____ men of the Roman Republic elected two leaders,

called _____. To make _____ on any public plan, both consuls

had to agree. The Romans also had a _____, which advised the consuls.

The Senate was a group of wealthy _____.

There were two _____ of citizens in the Roman Republic: _____

and plebeians. The patricians were wealthy men who _____ a lot of land.

They became consuls and _____. The _____ were ordinary

people. The slaves were the _____.

In 264 B.C., Rome began the _____ Wars. The Punic Wars were against

_____, a rival city in Northern Africa. There were three difficult wars, but

the _____ finally defeated Carthage in _____ B.C. With its victory,

Rome became the _____ most powerful empire. It lasted for almost

_____ years.

B **Write the meaning of each word or phrase from Word List in English.**

1	半島	_____	8	地主	_____
2	鄰近的	_____	9	階級	_____
3	驅逐	_____	10	貴族	_____
4	共和政體	_____	11	平民	_____
5	選舉	_____	12	布匿戰爭	_____
6	執政官	_____	13	迦太基	_____
7	元老院	_____	14	競爭的	_____

10 The Founding of Rome

A Listen to the passage and fill in the blanks.   🎧 46

_____ says that Rome was founded in _____ B.C. by Romulus and Remus.

Romulus and Remus were _____ brothers. The father of these two boys was not a man but _____, the Roman god of war. And their mother was the _____ Rhea Silvia. Their grandfather once was a king but had been _____.

When _____ and Remus were born, they were put into a basket and _____ into the Tiber River. The new king, Amulius, _____ that someday the boys might overthrow him.

Luckily, the basket _____ to the edge of the river, and the boys were _____ by a mother wolf. She took care of the babies _____ _____ they were her own. Later, a _____ took the boys and raised them.

When the boys _____ _____, they learned about their history. They killed _____ and made their grandfather king again.

Romulus and _____ decided to build their own city. But they _____ over many things. During one _____ argument, Romulus killed Remus. Romulus finished building his city on the seven hills on the _____ River. He _____ the city Rome after himself.

B Write the meaning of each word or phrase from Word List in English.

1 傳說   _____
2 建立   _____
3 女祭司   _____
4 推翻   _____
5 被丟入……   _____
6 害怕   _____
7 援救   _____
8 猶如   _____
9 牧羊人   _____
10 養育   _____
11 爭吵   _____
12 嚴重的   _____
13 爭執   _____
14 以……的名字命名 _____

11 Europe in the Middle Ages

A Listen to the passage and fill in the blanks. ∩ 47

The Roman Empire _____ in 476. The Romans had _____ all the land along the coast of the Mediterranean Sea and in most parts of _____. By the 300s and _____, the Roman Empire had _____ too big for one man to rule, so it was split in two: the _____ Roman Empire and the Eastern Roman Empire.

The Western Roman Empire was conquered by _____ invaders in 476. But the Eastern Roman Empire, also known as the _____ Empire, lasted until _____. We call the _____ between the fall of Western Roman Empire and the 1400s the Middle Ages.

The early _____ _____ are often called "the Dark Ages" because few Europeans could read or write. For most _____, life during this time was hard and dangerous. Many people died of war, hunger, and _____. However, for the _____ Church, the Middle Ages were a time of _____. Christianity became the _____ religion of the Roman Empire under Emperor _____ in 313, and it continued to _____ even after the Western Roman Empire fell. By the year 800, Charlemagne _____ much of Western Europe and _____ Christianity wherever his troops went. Eventually, the church _____ wealthy and powerful.

B Write the meaning of each word or phrase from Word List in English.

1 瓦解 _____
2 分裂 _____
3 日耳曼民族的 _____
4 侵略者 _____
5 拜占庭帝國 _____
6 法定的；正式的 _____
7 君士坦丁大帝 _____
8 查理曼大帝 _____
9 軍隊 _____
10 最後 _____

A Listen to the passage and fill in the blanks. 🎧 48

During the Middle Ages, a _____ social system called feudalism arose. It

was mostly _____ in England, France, and Germany.

In _____, land was exchanged for service. In many places, kings

_____ their land into fiefs. _____ were large areas of land controlled

by the local _____. A lord divided his fief among his _____. The

vassals _____ smaller fiefs of their own. The vassals were _____

to keep their fiefs only as long as they _____ served their king or lord.

Vassals, lords, and kings swore _____ to keep these rules.

One way a vassal _____ his lord or king was by providing _____ when

they were needed. Knights _____ loyalty to their lord and their king. In

battle, they wore metal _____ and often fought on horseback.

At the bottom of feudal society were the small farmers called _____, or

peasants. Serfs had few _____. They had to work on the _____

owned by the lords. They could not move away from a manor without the lord's

_____.

B Write the meaning of each word or phrase from Word List in English.

1 封建制度 _____
2 實行 _____
3 采邑;封地 _____
4 領主 _____
5 附庸;封臣 _____
6 忠實地 _____
7 宣誓 _____
8 誓言 _____
9 騎士 _____
10 盔甲 _____
11 騎著馬的;在馬背上的 _____
12 農奴 _____
13 僱農 _____
14 莊園;莊園大屋 _____
15 離開 _____
16 准許 _____

13 What Is the Scientific Method?

A Listen to the passage and fill in the blanks.

Do you sometimes ask "why" _____ when you are _____ about the things around you? _____ often ask questions about things in our world, too. When scientists want to answer a question, they use _____ skills called the scientific method. The scientific _____ is a way that scientists use to solve a problem and to _____ _____ how things work. Scientists often use the _____ five steps in the scientific method.

❶ _____ **and Question**

Scientists _____ things carefully and ask a question. Asking and answering questions is the _____ of inquiry.

❷ **Hypothesis**

Scientists make a _____ based on what they observe. A good _____ must be testable with an experiment.

❸ **Experiment**

The third step is to conduct _____. Experiments are very important for _____ the hypothesis.

❹ **Collecting and _____ Data**

Collecting and interpreting data are the _____ parts of an experiment. Scientists often use math _____ when they collect and interpret data.

❺ **Conclusion**

Now, it is time to draw a _____. Do the results _____ the hypothesis or not? If the hypothesis was not _____, scientists _____ another hypothesis and test it again.

B Write the meaning of each word or phrase from Word List in English.

1	好奇的		9	做出預測
2	詢問；質詢		10	根據
3	科學方法		11	可驗證的
4	想出（答案等）		12	實驗
5	觀察 (n.)		13	收集
6	觀察 (v.)		14	解釋；說明
7	基礎；準則		15	下結論
8	假設		16	支持

14 Scientific Tools

A Listen to the passage and fill in the blanks. 🎧 50

Scientists do much work in _____. These _____ are often filled

with all kinds of scientific tools and _____. Scientists use tools to

measure, observe, and _____ things.

To find the _____ of a liquid, scientists use a measuring cup, a _____,

or a graduated cylinder. A _____ measures temperature, a _____

measures weight, and a ruler measures length.

Sometimes scientists need to _____ an object closely. When they want

to observe _____, they might use a hand lens or a _____ glass.

These are small, _____ instruments that make objects _____

larger than they really are. For very small objects, scientists might use a

_____. A microscope _____ an object and makes it look

several times bigger than it is.

Scientists _____ or pick up tiny objects with _____. And, when they

need to heat something, they will _____ use a Bunsen _____.

Finally, safety is _____ important in a laboratory. So, scientists often

wear lab coats, _____, and gloves to protect their _____. These are

important tools, too.

B Write the meaning of each word or phrase from Word List in English.

1 實驗室 _____
2 充滿 _____
3 操作 _____
4 量杯 _____
5 量筒 _____
6 放大鏡 _____

7 手持的 _____
8 顯微鏡 _____
9 放大 _____
10 鑷子 _____
11 極端地 _____
12 實驗服 _____

15 What Are Cells?

A Listen to the passage and fill in the blanks. 🎧51

Cells are the basic _____ of life. All living things are made of _____. Big or

small, every organism is made of _____ _____ one or more cells.

Plant and animal cells have many of the same _____. All cells have a

_____, the control center of the cell. The outer _____ of a cell is

the cell _____. And both plant and animal cells are filled with

_____.

But plant cells _____ in some ways. Plant cells have cell walls, which is the

_____ layer outside the cell membrane. Another important part of plants is

_____. Chloroplasts contain _____. It gives plants their

green color and _____ them undergo _____.

Many animals' cells have _____ purposes. For instance, some cells can

come together to form _____ such as muscles. They can also create

_____ such as the heart, liver, lungs, and _____. These organs all

have important _____ in animals' bodies.

B Write the meaning of each word or phrase from Word List in English.

1	單位	_____	9	硬的	_____
2	細胞	_____	10	葉綠體	_____
3	細胞核	_____	11	葉綠素	_____
4	外面的	_____	12	光合作用	_____
5	覆蓋物	_____	13	專門的	_____
6	細胞膜	_____	14	（動植物的）組織	_____
7	細胞質	_____	15	器官	_____
8	細胞壁	_____	16	腎臟	_____

16 Classifying Living Things

A Listen to the passage and fill in the blanks. ∩ 52

There are _____ _____ types of animals and plants on Earth. The basic
unit of all _____ is the cell. Some organisms are only _____ of
one cell while others, like _____, are made up of billions of different
cells.

Organisms are grouped by _____ they have in common. One way to
_____ organisms is the cells. Scientists often compare one-celled
organisms to _____ organisms.

The smallest organisms on Earth are _____, or microscopic
organisms. They are so small that a person cannot see them without using a
_____. Many microorganisms are _____ organisms. Bacteria,
viruses, and _____ are three different types of microorganisms. They
have everything that they need to live in a _____ cell.

Most organisms have _____ _____ one cell. We call _____
multi-celled organisms. _____, fish, amphibians, mammals, and birds
are all multi-celled organisms. _____ and plants are also multi-celled
organisms.

B Write the meaning of each word or phrase from Word List in English.

1 由⋯⋯構成 _____f_____   7 單細胞的 _____

2 人類 _____   8 多細胞的 _____

3 由⋯⋯組成 _____m_____   9 微生物 _____

4 共同的；共有的 _____   10 微小的；用顯微鏡才能看見的 _____

5 將⋯⋯分類 _____   11 原生生物 _____

6 比較 _____   12 真菌；菌類植物 _____

Daily Test 17 What Is Heredity?

Have you ever _____ why you look like your parents? _____ you have the same eye _____ as your father. Or perhaps you and your mother have _____ noses. The reason for these _____ is heredity. Heredity is the _____ _____ of certain traits from parents to their offspring.

The basic unit of _____ is the gene. Genes carry _____ for how an organism will grow and develop. Every human has the same number of _____, but the instructions on the genes vary. That is why every human has different _____.

Genes are _____ from parents to offspring when a _____ _____ and an egg cell join. This means half of the _____ material comes from the mother, and half comes from the father. So the children will _____ the traits of both of their parents.

However, there are two _____ _____ genes. They are _____ and recessive genes. Dominant genes are _____ than recessive genes. _____ genes are in the body, but they do not do anything. Dominant genes are the ones that actually _____ an organism's traits and appearance.

B Write the meaning of each word or phrase from Word List in English.

1	對……感到疑惑；想知道 _____	10	基因 _____
2	看起來像…… _____	11	指示 _____
3	或許 _____	12	變化 _____
4	看起來相似的 _____	13	精細胞 _____
5	相似點 _____	14	卵細胞 _____
6	遺傳 _____	15	基因的；遺傳的 _____
7	傳下來 _____	16	經遺傳而獲得（性格、特徵等）_____
8	特徵 _____	17	顯性基因 _____
9	後代；子女 _____	18	隱性基因 _____

18 What Are Traits?

A Listen to the passage and fill in the blanks. 🎧 54

A trait is a particular _____ that organisms have. All organisms have different _____. Some traits are _____ only by genes. However, some traits develop _____ a combination of genes and nurture. We can divide the traits into two groups: _____ traits and learned traits. Inherited traits are characteristics that come from your _____. For humans, eye color, hair color, and the shape of the _____ are all inherited traits. The great size of elephants and the spots of _____ are other inherited traits. Organisms cannot _____ their inherited traits. These traits are _____ only by the genes passed down from their parents. However, _____ traits are different. _____ and the environment can influence many traits. You cannot change your _____ _____, but you can change some characteristics by the way you _____. For instance, you might change your _____. If you eat healthy food and _____, your body can grow taller than your _____ information. Knowing how to read and how to ride a _____ are also learned traits.

B Write the meaning of each word or phrase from Word List in English.

1 特徵　　_____
2 特性　　_____
3 影響　　_____
4 結合　　_____
5 養育；教養　_____

6 遺傳特徵　_____
7 習得特徵　_____
8 改變　　_____
9 由……所決定　_____
10 基因資訊　_____

A Listen to the passage and fill in the blanks. 🎧 55

Around _____ _____ years ago, the earth formed. During that time, the planet has _____ many changes. _____ have divided the history of the earth into different _____ _____. This is called the _____ time scale. The geologic time scale is divided into several _____. Each era is an _____ long period of time.

The _____ Era was the first. It _____ about 90% of all the earth's history. It covered the time from Earth's _____ to about 600 million years ago. During this time, the earth was still extremely hot since it was just _____. Also, the earth's _____ began to gain oxygen, and plants and animals started to develop.

Next was the _____ Era. It lasted for around _____ million years. Earth's oxygen level _____. Invertebrates, fish, and reptiles _____ during it.

The _____ Era lasted for around 150 million years. This era is often known as the age of the _____. Dinosaurs _____ this period, but small mammals began to evolve.

Today, we live in the _____ Era. It has _____ for about 65 million years. Scientists often refer to it as the time of _____.

B Write the meaning of each word or phrase from Word List in English.

1	四十五億年	9	古生代
2	經歷	10	穩定
3	時期	11	無脊椎動物
4	地質學的	12	演化；進化
5	時間表；年代表	13	中生代
6	時代；【地】代	14	主宰
7	前寒武紀時代	15	新生代
8	包含	16	稱……為……

20 Continental Drift

A Listen to the passage and fill in the blanks. 🎧56

Today, there are seven _____ on the earth. But the earth's _____

did not always look this way. Scientists believe that millions of years ago, there

was just one _____ on the entire Earth. It was called _____.

Scientists also _____ that the continents joined together and then

_____ _____ at several times in the earth's history.

How did it _____? The _____ is explained by a theory of

continental drift. The _____ explains that Earth's continents move very

slowly from one _____ to another.

The continents are all on the earth's _____. There are many huge

_____ that make up the crust. The crust is _____. However,

_____ it is the mantle. Much of the mantle is hot, _____ _____

which can flow like a liquid. This melted rock _____ the crust above it. So

the plates are _____ in motion. Even today, the continents move a few

_____ every year.

As a result, the earth's surface is _____ changing. If these changes

_____, the earth's surface will look very different in another million

years.

B Write the meaning of each word or phrase from Word List in English.

1 超大陸 _____ 7 地殼 _____

2 假定 _____ 8 板塊 _____

3 拉開；拆開 _____ 9 地函 _____

4 謎 _____ 10 熔岩 _____

5 學說；理論 _____ 11 不斷地 _____

6 大陸漂移 _____ 12 持續地 _____

21 Light and Heat

A Listen to the passage and fill in the blanks. ∩ 57

Light is a form of _____ that moves in waves. Light _____ move

_____ kilometers every second, so they are faster than everything in the

_____. On Earth, the main _____ of light is the sun.

Light can be both _____ and refracted. Light travels in _____

lines until it hits something. When light hits an object, the light _____

_____ the surface of the object. You can see your _____ because light

bounces off the _____ and back to you. That is _____.

_____ occurs when light goes through an object, such as water, and

the light _____.

_____ is another form of energy. Heat moves through _____,

convection, and radiation. Conduction is the movement of heat by matter

to _____ it. Some materials, such as metals, _____ heat well.

Convection is the movement of heat in a _____ liquid or gas. Ovens work

by _____. Finally, _____ is the movement of heat without

matter to carry it. The sun sends out heat _____ radiation.

B Write the meaning of each word or phrase from Word List in English.

1 光波 _____   7 彎曲 _____
2 反射 (v.) _____   8 傳導 (n.) _____
3 折射 (v.) _____   9 對流 _____
4 反射；彈回 _____   10 輻射 _____
5 反射 (n.) _____   11 傳導 (v.) _____
6 折射 (n.) _____   12 加熱的；受熱的 _____

22 Electricity

A Listen to the passage and fill in the blanks. 🎧 58

_____ is a form of energy. There are _____ electricity and current electricity.

Static electricity is an _____ charge that builds up on an object by _____ or friction. Static electricity is _____ and somewhat unpredictable. Current electricity is a _____ stream of charges. _____ electricity is more useful than static electricity because it can be more _____ controlled. Current electricity runs through _____.

Let's light a _____ by using an electric circuit. A _____ is the path that an _____ current follows. The electric current moves along a path that _____ the battery and bulb. The bulb _____ only when the wire _____ it to the battery is closed. The battery _____ energy to the circuit. We call this a _____ circuit. An open circuit does not _____ electricity to flow.

A _____ circuit is a circuit that has only one _____ for a current to follow. A _____ circuit is a circuit that has more than one path for a current to _____.

B Write the meaning of each word or phrase from Word List in English.

1 靜電	_____	8 電路	_____
2 電流	c_____	9 電流	e_____
3 電荷	_____	10 連接	_____
4 短暫的	_____	11 閉合電路；閉路	_____
5 不可預測的	_____	12 開路；斷路	_____
6 穩定的	_____	13 串聯電路	_____
7 電燈泡	_____	14 並聯電路	_____

23 Motion and Force

A Listen to the passage and fill in the blanks. 🎧 59

Everything in the universe _____. The sun, Earth, the _____, and even all of the stars in the universe are in _____ motion.

All objects in motion have _____. This is the _____ speed of a moving object. The position of an object is its _____. Moving objects have constantly changing _____.

According to the _____ of motion discovered by Sir Isaac _____, an object in motion will continue at the same _____ and in the same direction until it is _____ _____ by an outside force. This is known as the law of _____.

One outside _____ is gravity. _____ is the force of attraction between Earth and other _____. It pulls things _____ Earth.

_____ is the force that acts between any two objects and _____ them to _____ one another. Gravitation helps hold Earth in its _____ around the sun. The other planets, too, are _____ in their orbits by gravitation.

_____ is another force that can _____ _____ or stop moving objects. When two _____ rub together, they create friction.

B Write the meaning of each word or phrase from Word List in English.

1 速度 _____
2 速率 _____
3 位置 _____
4 力 _____
5 慣性定律 _____

6 地心引力 _____
7 萬有引力 _____
8 軌道 _____
9 摩擦力 _____
10 摩擦 _____

24 Simple Machines

A Listen to the passage and fill in the blanks. 🎧 60

We live in an _____ _____ machines. Machines are _____ that do

work. Many modern machines are _____. But most are based on simple

_____. A simple machine has very few _____ but makes it easier

for people to move things. There are six _____ of them.

An _____ _____ is a kind of ramp. It makes _____ up or down

something easier.

A _____ is two inclined planes placed _____ ____ _____. It can

_____ something in place, _____ something, or split something. A

_____ is a wedge.

A _____ is used to hold two objects together and to _____ them from

_____ _____.

A _____ is a simple bar that we use to move objects by _____ force at

another point. _____ and pliers are levers.

A _____ is a wheel with a _____ _____ that can carry a line.

Pulleys, like _____, are useful for lifting heavy objects.

A wheel and _____ is a kind of lever. It has a wheel that is connected to a

_____ called an axle. A wheel and axle changes the strength of a _____

_____ and makes work easier. Doorknobs and _____ are

examples of a wheel and axle.

B Write the meaning of each word or phrase from Word List in English.

1	裝置 _____	9	使用；施用 _____
2	複雜的 _____	10	鉗子 _____
3	斜面 _____	11	滑輪 _____
4	斜面；斜坡 _____	12	表面有溝槽的 _____
5	楔子 _____	13	框邊 _____
6	背對背 _____	14	輪軸 _____
7	螺旋 _____	15	軸 _____
8	槓桿 _____	16	球形門把 _____

25 Understanding Fractions

A Listen to the passage and fill in the blanks. 🎧 61

A fraction is a number that _____ a part of a whole.

In the picture, each _____ _____ of the whole is $\frac{1}{4}$. We call the fraction _____ a unit fraction. A unit fraction has a _____ of 1.

When the numerator of a _____ is greater than or equal to the _____, we call it an _____ fraction. $\frac{5}{5}$, $\frac{4}{3}$, and _____ are all improper fractions. Improper fractions can be written as either _____ _____ or mixed numbers. The _____ in a fraction means the same as a _____ sign. So, the fraction _____ means the same thing as _____. 5÷5=1. Therefore, the fraction $\frac{5}{5}$ _____ the whole number 1. $\frac{4}{3}$ = _____, so $\frac{4}{3}$ can be written as the mixed number _____.

Some fractions, such as $\frac{1}{2}$ and _____, name the same amount. $\frac{1}{2}=\frac{3}{6}$. Such fractions are called _____ fractions. You can make an equivalent fraction by _____ or dividing the numerator and denominator by _____ _____ number. $\frac{1}{2} = \frac{1\times3}{2\times3} = \frac{3}{6}$ $\frac{3}{6} = \frac{3\div3}{6\div3} = \frac{1}{2}$

A fraction is in its _____ form when its numerator and denominator have no _____ _____ greater than 1. A common factor is a number that the _____ and denominator can both be divided by. For example, $\frac{4}{8} = \frac{4\div4}{8\div4} = \frac{1}{2}$. So, 4 is a common factor of 4 and ____. The simplest form of _____ is $\frac{1}{2}$.

The largest number that can _____ both the numerator and the denominator is called the greatest common factor. For example, _____ can be divided by both 2 and 4. $\frac{12}{16} = \frac{12\div2}{16\div2} = \frac{6}{8}$ or $\frac{12}{16} = \frac{12\div4}{16\div4} = \frac{3}{4}$

2 and 4 are common factors, and 4 is the _____ common factor of 12 and ____.

B Write the meaning of each word or phrase from Word List in English.

1 陳述	_____	7 整數	_____
2 等分	_____	8 帶分數	_____
3 單位分數	_____	9 除號	_____
4 分子	_____	10 等值分數	_____
5 分母	_____	11 公因數	_____
6 假分數	_____	12 最簡分數	_____

26 Word Problems With Fractions

A Listen to the passage and fill in the blanks. 🎧 62

1. What are the common factors and the _____ common factor of _____?

   Solution: $\frac{16÷2}{20÷2} = \frac{8}{10}$. $\frac{16÷4}{20÷4} = \frac{4}{5}$.

   Since $\frac{16}{20}$ can be _____ by both 2 and 4, 2 and 4 are common factors

   of 16 and _____. And 4 is the greatest _____ _____ of $\frac{16}{20}$.

2. _____ the fraction $\frac{12}{18}$ to its simplest form.

   Solution 1: Divide the numerator and _____ by 2.

   $\frac{12}{18} = \frac{12÷2}{18÷2} = \frac{6}{9}$.

   Since $\frac{6}{9}$ is not in its _____ form, you can go further. Divide the

   numerator and denominator _____ __. $\frac{6÷3}{9÷3} = \frac{2}{3}$.

   There are no more common factors _____ _____ 1. So, the

   simplest form of _____ $= \frac{2}{3}$.

   Solution 2: _____ the numerator and denominator by the greatest

   common factor. Then you can find the simplest form in _____ _____.

   $\frac{12÷6}{18÷6} = \frac{2}{3}$. So, the simplest form of $\frac{12}{18} = \frac{2}{3}$.

3. _____ the fractions $\frac{2}{5}$ and _____.

   Solution: $\frac{2}{5} < \frac{4}{5}$. $\frac{4}{5}$ is greater than $\frac{2}{5}$.

   When you compare fractions with common _____, you only

   compare the numerators.

4. Compare the fractions $\frac{2}{3}$ and _____.

   Solution: $\frac{2}{3} = \frac{2×2}{3×2} = \frac{4}{6}$. $\frac{4}{6} > \frac{3}{6}$.

   So, $\frac{2}{3}$ is greater than $\frac{3}{6}$. To compare _____ _____, you need

   to make their denominators the same. Therefore, find the _____

   fraction for $\frac{2}{3}$ with a denominator of 6 first. Once their denominators are the

   same, you can _____ compare them.

B Write the meaning of each word or ph1rase from Word List in English.

1 最大公因數 _____

2 解答 _____

3 約分 _____

4 一步到位 _____

5 公分母 _____

6 異分母分數 _____

A Listen to the passage and fill in the blanks. 🎧 63

When two lines, line _____, or _____ meet at a common point,

they form an angle. The point where they come together is called a _____.

Here is _____ ABC.

_____ B is the vertex of angle ABC. It can be _____ like this, too:

∠ABC or ∠CBA. When you _____ an angle, you always put the vertex in

the middle.

The size of an angle is measured in _____(°). When we measure angles,

we use a measuring tool called a _____. An angle can measure

anywhere from 0 to _____ degrees.

There are four types of _____. A right angle _____ exactly 90°.

A right angle forms when _____ lines intersect. An _____

angle is less than a right angle. It measures greater than ____ and less than 90°.

An _____ angle is greater than a right angle. It measures greater than

_____ and less than 180°. A _____ angle measures 180°. A straight

angle _____ a line.

B Write the meaning of each word or phrase from Word List in English.

1	線段	_____	7 直角	_____
2	射線	_____	8 垂直線	_____
3	角	_____	9 相交	_____
4	頂點	_____	10 銳角	_____
5	度	_____	11 鈍角	_____
6	量角器	_____	12 平角	_____

28 Polygons, Triangles, and Circles

A Listen to the passage and fill in the blanks. 🎧64

A polygon is a _____ _____ with three or more sides. A polygon with four _____ can be a square, rectangle, _____, rhombus, or trapezoid. A polygon with five sides is a _____, and one with six sides is a _____.

A _____ with three sides is a triangle. There are several types of _____. A triangle with three equal sides is an _____ triangle. A triangle with two equal sides is an _____ triangle. And a triangle with three sides that are all _____ is a _____ triangle.

Also, all the angles in an acute triangle are _____. A right triangle has one _____ angle. And an obtuse triangle has one _____ angle.

A _____ is a closed rounded figure in which every point is the same _____ from the center. Circles have different _____. A _____ is a line segment that connects two points on the circle. The _____ is a chord that bisects a circle. And the _____ is a line segment with one endpoint at the center of a circle and the other _____ on the circle. It is _____ the length of the diameter.

B Write the meaning of each word or phrase from Word List in English.

1	多邊形	_____	
2	封閉圖形	_____	
3	邊	_____	
4	平行四邊形	_____	
5	菱形	_____	
6	梯形	_____	
7	五邊形	_____	

8	六邊形	_____	
9	等邊三角形	_____	
10	等腰三角形	_____	
11	不等邊三角形	_____	
12	弦	_____	
13	直徑	_____	
14	半徑	_____	

29 Prefixes and Suffixes

A Listen to the passage and fill in the blanks. 🎧 65

Prefixes and suffixes are groups of _____ that are added to the _____ or ends of words. They often add _____ meanings to words and make new _____.

A _____ goes at the beginning of a word. There are many prefixes in _____. Some prefixes mean "no" or "not." _____ them are *im-*, *in-*, *un-*, *dis-*, and *non-*. For _____, *impossible* means "not possible," _____ means "not dependent," *unhappy* means "not happy," and *dishonest* means "not honest." Here are some _____ common prefixes and their _____:

pre-	= before	_____
fore-	= before, beforehand	_____, foreground
mid-	= middle	_____
inter-	= between, among	_____, international
re-	= again	_____, redo
mis-	= wrong, wrongly	_____, mistake

A _____ goes at the end of a word. There are many suffixes in English. Two very common suffixes are *-ed* and *-ing*. *-ed* makes the _____ _____ form of a verb. And *-ing* makes the _____ form of a verb. _____ some other common suffixes and their meanings:

-er	= a person who	teacher, _____
-en	= made of	_____
-ful	= full of	_____
-able	= able to be done	_____
-less	= without	_____, painless

It is useful to know _____ used prefixes and suffixes. Sometimes you can _____ _____ the meanings of some difficult words by _____ them down into prefixes, roots, and suffixes.

B Write the meaning of each word or phrase from Word List in English.

1 字首 _____	5 獨立的 _____	9 過去式 _____
2 字尾 _____	6 預習 _____	10 進行式 _____
3 額外的 _____	7 前景 _____	11 分解 _____
4 在……之中 _____	8 期中考 _____	12 字根 _____

30 Tenses

A Listen to the passage and fill in the blanks. 🎧 66

In English, all _____ have a verb. A verb shows the _____ in the sentence. Verbs can tell about actions that are _____ now, actions that happened before, and actions that will happen _____. We call this a _____. The tense shows the time in which an action _____ _____. There are three main _____ tenses: the past tense, the _____ tense, and the future tense.

The past tense _____ things that have already happened.

I _____ my friend yesterday.

She *lived* in New York City _____ _____ ago.

The present tense describes things that are _____ now. We also use the present tense to refer to repeated or _____ actions as well as to _____ facts.

I _____ _____ a house on Main Street.

I *get* up at _____ _____ in the morning.

Earth _____ the sun.

The _____ tense describes things that will _____ in the future.

I *will go* to school _____.

Mr. Taylor *is going to find* a new job _____ _____.

_____ are the three basic tenses. There are also different _____ ____ each tense: the continuous tense and _____ _____. We can use the past, present, and future _____ tenses. We can also use the _____, present, and future perfect tenses.

B Write the meaning of each word or phrase from Word List in English.

1 時態　　_____
2 發生　　_____
3 過去式　_____
4 現在式　_____
5 未來式　_____

6 描述　　_____
7 重複的；反覆的　_____
8 習慣的　_____
9 進行式　_____
10 完成式　_____

31

31 Complete Sentences

A Listen to the passage and fill in the blanks. 🎧 67

A sentence is a group of words that _____ a complete thought. A _____ sentence has a subject and a predicate. The _____ tells what the sentence is about. The _____ tells what the subject of the sentence is or _____.

Subject	Predicate
John	eats.
She	_____ TV.
My big brother	_____ _____ school every day.

The subject is usually a noun or a _____, and it usually comes ____ ____ _____ of the sentence. The predicate must _____ a verb and may include other parts of speech.

A sentence _____ is a part of a sentence or an _____ sentence. It is _____ either a subject or a verb, and it does not express a complete _____.

Sentence Fragment	Complete Sentence
Went to the movies	I went to the _____.
Movies last weekend	I went to the movies last _____.

A _____ sentence contains two or more complete sentences. The sentences are joined by a comma and a _____ like *and*, *but*, *so*, and *or*.

I like oranges, *and* my sister _____ oranges, too.
We stayed home, *but* James _____ _____.

If you do not use a _____ or a conjunction when you combine two sentences, you make a _____ sentence.

Run-on Sentence	Complete Sentence
Be careful don't move.	Be _____, and don't move.
I speak English John speaks Chinese.	I speak English, and John speaks _____.
	I speak English. John speaks Chinese.

B Write the meaning of each word or phrase from Word List in English.

1 完整句　_____
2 主詞　_____
3 述語　_____
4 代名詞　_____
5 詞性　_____

6 句子片斷；不完整句　_____
7 遺漏　_____
8 複合句　_____
9 連接詞　_____
10 連寫句；不斷句　_____

32 Proofreading

A Listen to the passage and fill in the blanks. 🎧 68

Read the _____ below. There are 9 _____ in the paragraph. Use _____ marks to correct the mistakes.

Proofreading Marks

went
~~go~~ Draw a line through each _____ word and write the correct word above it.

∧ _____ words and punctuation.

Delete incorrect words and _____.

≡ Capitalize a letter.

／ Lowercase a letter.

Jessica always does something _____ every weekend. Last Saturday, she decided to visit the _____ _____ with her friend Tina. Jessica and Tina _____ the bus to the amusement park. They got there _____ in the morning because there were _____ people there until _____. This way, they did not have to wait _____ _____ very long.

Jessica loves _____ _____, and so does Tina. They _____ on a couple of them, and then they rode on the _____ _____, too. They started to _____ _____, so they bought some _____ and drinks and sat down for a while. Jessica wanted to go on some more _____, but Tina didn't. The park was beginning to get _____, so they had to wait _____ to go on each ride. Jessica and Tina _____ to go home. They had a _____ day. They went to the _____ _____ and then rode back to their homes.

B Write the meaning of each word or phrase from Word List in English.

1 （文章的）段 _____
2 錯誤 _____
3 校對 _____
4 校對符號 _____
5 不正確的 _____
6 插入 _____
7 標點符號 _____
8 刪除 _____
9 用大寫書寫 _____
10 用小寫書寫 _____
11 遊樂園 _____
12 排隊 _____
13 疲倦 _____
14 人潮擁擠 _____

33 The Art of the Middle Ages

A Listen to the passage and fill in the blanks. 🎧69

The Middle Ages lasted for around _____ years until _____. During

this time, many _____ Gothic cathedrals were built in Europe, and

most art was _____ by the Church.

Many _____ cathedrals had towers and _____ that reached high

in the air. The height and grandeur of cathedrals _____ people to be more

religious. Tall ceilings, paintings, and _____ windows depicting stories

from the _____ also created awe-inspiring spaces.

Another feature of Gothic cathedrals was their _____. Because the

cathedrals were so tall and _____, stone braces called buttresses

_____ the cathedrals and kept them from collapsing. Stone statues of

_____ called gargoyles were often found on cathedrals, too. Notre Dame

Cathedral and Chartres _____ in France are two famous _____

cathedrals.

Some of the most beautiful medieval art is also found in books called

_____ manuscripts. During the Middle Ages, books were copied by

hand by _____. Monks illuminated many of the pages by _____

pictures with bits of real gold and silver in the books. *The Book of Kells* is one

famous illuminated _____.

B Write the meaning of each word or phrase from Word List in English.

1	中世紀	_____	9	惡魔	_____
2	雄偉的	_____	10	滴水獸	_____
3	哥德式的	_____	11	中世紀的	_____
4	大教堂	_____	12	（書籍等）用鮮明圖案裝飾的 _____
5	尖塔	_____			
6	激起；喚起	_____	13	手抄本；手稿	_____
7	令人肅然起敬的	_____	14	僧侶	_____
8	扶壁	_____	15	少許……；一些……	_____

34 The Art of Islam and Africa

A   Listen to the passage and fill in the blanks.   🎧 70

Art from around the world has _____ styles and looks.

During the Middle Ages, _____ from North Africa conquered much of

Spain. They developed a very different _____ style from the Gothic

style.

One of the main features of _____ architecture is the minaret. Most

_____ —Islamic houses of worship—have four _____. These

are tall towers found at each of the four _____ of a mosque. Many Islamic

buildings have _____, too. A dome is a rounded roof or a _____ on

a building. The Dome of the Rock in _____, Israel, and the Taj Mahal in

Agra, India, are two beautiful _____ of Islamic architecture.

In Africa, artists made both _____ and masks. A long time ago, many

African people did not write down their _____. They _____

things from the past by singing songs, dancing, and making _____ of art.

To remember their _____, they carved sculptures and made many

_____. The sculptures were _____ made of terra cotta or brass.

They _____ people and animals. The masks showed various _____.

African people wore them when they _____ mask dances.

B   **Write the meaning of each word or phrase from Word List in English.**

1   穆斯林；伊斯蘭教徒 _____

2   建築   _____

3   清真寺   _____

4   喚拜塔；叫拜樓（清真寺的尖塔）

               _____

5   雕像   _____

6   祖先   _____

7   典型地   _____

8   赤陶土   _____

9   黃銅   _____

10   面具舞   _____

11   描繪   _____

35 Musical Notation

A Listen to the passage and fill in the blanks. ∩ 71

People around the world, _____ _____ language they speak,

can read music and sing or play it. This is all _____ _____ musical notation.

Songwriters and _____ use a special kind of writing called "notation"

to write down their music. Once you can read the _____, you can freely

sing and play music no matter how _____ it is.

Let's look at some _____ _____ musical notation. Musical notes are written

on a _____. The notes basically tell us the _____, length, and pitch of

the music. Sometimes, a musical note may have a _____ over it. We call it a

_____ note. It tells the _____ to increase the length of the note by

one half. Sometimes, there is a _____ _____ connecting two notes.

This line is called a _____. It tells the musician to continue to _____ the first

note _____ the time of the second.

At the beginning of each _____ _____ music is the time _____.

It is always two numbers, such as $\frac{4}{4}$, $\frac{3}{4}$, or _____. The time signature shows the

_____ or beat of the piece and _____ how the musician should

play it.

Composers often divide their music into _____. To show where a

measure begins and _____, they use a single _____ _____. To show

where a piece of music is _____, they use a double bar line.

B Write the meaning of each word or phrase from Word List in English.

1 無論什麼   _____   7 附點音符   _____

2 讀樂譜   _____   8 連結線   _____

3 樂譜   _____   9 拍號   _____

4 詞曲創作人   _____   10 小節   _____

5 作曲家   _____   11 節拍   _____

6 五線譜   _____   12 雙小節線   _____

36 Composers and Their Music

A Listen to the passage and fill in the blanks. 🎧 72

There have been many _____ composers of classical music. Three

of them are Johann Sebastian _____, George Friedrich Handel, and Joseph

Haydn.

Bach was a German composer and _____ from the Baroque Period. He

composed _____ works of music, including organ music,

_____, cantatas, and a lot of _____ music for the church. The

Brandenburg Concertos and *St. Matthew Passion* are some of his _____

works.

_____ was another German _____ composer. However, Handel

mostly lived in England and composed music with English _____. Handel is

best known for his _____ based on stories from the Bible. The

famous *Messiah*, which is performed by an orchestra and a _____, is one

of these pieces. It includes the *Hallelujah Chorus*, one of the most _____

works in all classical music.

_____ lived after Bach and Handel during the _____ Period. He is

sometimes called the Father of the _____. He composed more than

one _____ symphonies. *The Surprise Symphony* and *The Creation* are his

best-known _____. People also remember him for being the teacher

of Ludwig van _____, one of the greatest of all classical composers.

B Write the meaning of each word or phrase from Word List in English.

1 傑出的 _____
2 為數眾多的 _____
3 合唱音樂 _____
4 最著名的 _____
5 歌詞 _____
6 樂曲 _____
7 根據 _____
8 合唱團 _____

MEMO